I've travelled the world twice over,
Met the famous: saints and sinners,
Poets and artists, kings and queens,
Old stars and hopeful beginners,
I've been where no-one's been before,
Learned secrets from writers and cooks
All with one library ticket
To the wonderful world of books.

GOODBYE, NANNY GRAY

When Nanny Gray's body is discovered by two children, their quiet village is disturbed by rumour. Superintendent Bone is called in to investigate and is surprised at the number of potential murderers of this elderly and harmless woman. She has apparently been useful to so many, but has angered quite a few. Superintendent Bone has numerous leads to follow, all possible, all equally likely, in this classic English detective mystery.

JILL STAYNES and
MARGARET STOREY

GOODBYE, NANNY GRAY

Complete and Unabridged

ULVERSCROFT
Leicester

First published in Great Britain in 1987 by
The Bodley Head Ltd.,
London

First Large Print Edition
published August 1990
by arrangement with
The Bodley Head Ltd.,
London

British Library CIP Data

Staynes, Jill
    Goodbye, Nanny Gray.—Large print ed.—
Ulverscroft large print series: mystery
I. Title II. Storey, Margaret, *1926–*
823'.914[F]

    ISBN 0-7089-2261-9

Published by
F. A. Thorpe (Publishing) Ltd.
Anstey, Leicestershire
Set by Rowland Phototypesetting Ltd.
Bury St. Edmunds, Suffolk
Printed and bound in Great Britain by
T. J. Press (Padstow) Ltd., Padstow, Cornwall

1

SOMEWHERE in the forest a bird was making a noise like a watch being wound up. The pierrot stopped for a moment and listened, and then bent again to what lay at its feet. Bodies are heavier when there is no life in them and it was not easy work. The leaves underfoot rustled like animals moving, and there were roots and pieces of fallen branch that got in the way. The light of the moon, obscured from time to time behind quick-moving clouds, shone on the white satin coat and the black pom-poms with a soft radiance wasted on its observers. A fox on its way back to its den stared at the scene without making any more sense of it than it had to; the smell was human and the whole business best avoided. To the pierrot, whose arms and back were aching by now, the smell was equally strong, but what was perceived was the unfamiliar: wet leaves, autumnal decay of all kinds, and rot disturbed. At last a good place was

1

reached, far enough from the tracks that dissected the forest, and the burden was deposited, to add its own smell in time. As the pierrot returned, the cone hat shining softly through the trees, the bird angrily wound up its watch again and went back to sleep.

It was, of course, before this that the hand forced the paperweight down the side of the carton. This carton was near the rubbish bin which had first offered itself as a hiding place but whose contents would not bear touching. The carton was clean, and seemed to contain, at the top, old magazines and, lower down, old clothes. The hider replaced the large plastic bag that covered it, and was gone.

It was the children, or perhaps the dog, who found the body. The dog barked from a couple of yards' distance, defying his fear, shaking himself almost off the ground with each explosion. The children veered off their narrow path and crashed down kicking up beechmast and loam, into the hollow.

"Is it her, then?"

The boy, longer-legged and reckless down the slope, crouched over the long rag doll of clothes and limbs. The terrier fell warily silent and circled them.

"Course it's her. Cooh! It's not nice, don't look," but he stared, and she crowded close.

"It's her clothes all right. Looks all flat."

"Take the leaves off her face."

"Why me? You do it."

Neither of them reached out to do it. Both gazed with honest fascination, and with the sense that they were looking at what grown-ups would keep from them.

"I told you she was dead," the girl said. "She didn't look like that before. How'd she get here?"

"Walked, silly."

A small gust of wind obligingly twirled the leaves all round, baring the face. Both children came suddenly to their feet and he stumbled backwards, saying "Yeach!" Her hand gripped her mouth. They eyed the body now askance.

"There's been animals," the girl said.

"We have to tell the police."

"Yeh. Come on." She set off up the

3

slope, then paused. "Don't someone have to stay with it—her?"

They hesitated.

"Who's going to move anything?"

Relieved, they set off the way they had come. The dog, who had nervously been marking a young tree, circled the body and joined them. They all looked back.

"Did you see any dead person before?" she demanded.

"No."

"Not in going round the world and that?"

"No. They didn't have any. I've seen funerals, but they don't show the bodies then."

"I've seen them before." The girl's voice also gained confidence as they moved away. "I've seen them laid out. I've seen my nana, and Mrs. Beach, and *her*—" she jerked her head back—"and lots more."

"Bet you weren't supposed to."

"I can always get where I want. Nobody stops me."

"Oh, you're marvellous, you are."

"We both are. We're clever. We found her and the police didn't. They didn't look up here yet."

4

"Let's go to the phone box. We can dial nine nine nine. I always wanted to."

"Let me. It's not fair."

"I'll dial nine, nine, then you nine. OK?"

"Trying to make more holes in the Aubusson?"

The sarcasm in the voice was tired, as if its object had grown impervious; and, indeed, he stopped to peer at the carpet as though her question had been merely factual. She remembered, when he straightened again and put back the sweep of blond hair behind his ear, that she had once found him deeply attractive. She went on: "She'll turn up somewhere, in her own good time. Her time, I seem to think, was always better than anyone else's."

"You never liked Nanny."

She was amused by the accusation. "*I* never liked Nanny! *You* didn't actually adore her. Especially since Gareth died."

"It's ridiculous! Giving away our money —the family money—to her like that. How are we supposed to keep things up?"

"I don't think Gareth cared if we kept

things, as you put it, up or let them drop in the shit. He'd been in the shit for years."

Val threw his fist against the chimney-piece, scoring a hit on the marble eye of the lion supporting the Herne coat of arms. "That was his own doing. He'd no right to make a mess of our lives too."

"Weren't we doing rather well on our own?" She watched him nurse his bruised hand and walk away to look out of the window.

"There's the land. At one time I thought he cared about that."

She flicked the pages of the craft catalogue, impatiently. "Try the sobstuff on Nanny. I'm the audience that's sat through this for a month's performances already, remember?"

He turned, with a curious look on his face, whether desperation or laughter she could not tell.

"But I may never have a chance to talk to Nanny again."

"She's gone missing before."

"Not like this."

"She's just getting better at going missing."

He shot a vicious look at her. "You never take anything seriously. The police have been called in this time. I wouldn't be surprised," he toyed with the idea delicately, like a delicious dish one delays eating, "I wouldn't be surprised if none of us saw Nanny again."

"You'd have lost your chance then."

"Chance?" He looked genuinely surprised.

"Of persuading the old thing to cough up the family dough. Why didn't you go to see her more when you could have?"

"There was no point. She never liked me."

"You were all for going to persuade her a week ago."

He didn't bother to reply. He was arranging his hair once more. Gareth had never had such good looks as his younger brother. He gazed in the looking-glass and touched his tie. He was always odd, she remarked to herself, about Nanny, at one minute seeming to need her and talking of his childhood when life had been so secure and she was the centre of that security; and the next spiteful, impatient with the

7

signs of age in her, callous about her health.

"I suppose Nanny's money—our money, as you call it—will go to Carey Sidgwick," she said.

His reflection smiled at her. Mirrors made all smiles look lopsided. "Carey wants that money all right."

"You mean, some sort of trouble she's in?" Gossip was always fun.

"How should I know?" Suddenly indifferent, he shrugged and turned. "We shall have to wait until the police find her or her body."

"Poor old Nanny! You've got her buried already."

At that he came over to her and treated her to the view she once could never tire of; he crouched at her knee, raising those long-lashed blue eyes. His hand touched hers on the catalogue.

"You know how worried I am about everything. Can't help seeing everything in a nasty light. You've got to help me."

He was offering the blond hair for a stroke, so she indulged him. "It was what I married you for. Nanny'll turn up all right."

8

"Oh I do hope so. I do hope so."

Dr. West pushed the prescription across the desk, and Carey Sidgwick, picking it up, dropped it to the floor and had to dive for it. She sat up, folded the paper and smoothed it between finger and thumb. The paper trembled.

"If they could find her. Or if she'd phone me. I don't know . . ."

He wondered what caused this overreaction. She was a calm young woman as a rule; must be fonder of old Miss Gray than he had realised. One didn't know people . . . He was going to be late on his rounds and there was a heavy list this morning.

"Look, Carey. You know she's done this before. Of course you're anxious, particularly when you think she'd hit her head. It was naughty of you not to insist on a good look at it. Yes, yes, I do know what she could be like. Now, you have your job to think of. You must look after yourself, keep busy and not let worry get hold of you."

"But suppose she's ill . . ."

"She's a very tough old person."

She shot him a brown amazed glance.

9

To Carey Sidgwick, a woman Phoebe Gray's age must appear far too ancient to be tough.

"She is, you know. You mustn't overreact."

"No. No. I try not to be stupid."

As he hit the bell for the next patient, Dr. West wished he wasn't worried about Phoebe Gray's disappearance himself. She was not in fact so very strong. Not up to those walkabouts she went in for. Suppose she had hit her head?

"Where's the kid, then?"

Mrs. Stavely thumped the plate down in front of Ted Larkin. "Dawdling, as usual."

"Don't want her disappearing along of Nanny Gray." He already talked through baked beans.

"Don't you say that. She's trouble enough with her stories."

He reached out an arm like a tree branch across her way, and looked up. After an impatient shove at the barrier, she frowned at him. He was smiling as he chewed.

"Pack it in, Ted. Let me get on—"

"What'll you pay?"

"I'll give you what for if you don't."

He pivoted his chair from the table and dumped her on his knee. As she struggled, she glanced distractedly at the door. "Shut up, Ted, now. Mona'll be back any minute."

"Mona knows. She's not daft. Not as daft as she looks."

"That's enough from you." She was angry, and he heard the note and let her go. In any case he wanted his tea. She said, as she set up the ironing board with a thump and a clash, "Mona's got a strong imagination. That's all. She makes things up."

"She tells lies. Look what she said about old Ma Gray. Saw her lying dead in her bed. That's imagination. That is, all right." He stuffed his mouth and went on, "Time that old bitch fell off the perch. She must be a hundred; hundred years of minding other people's business and ordering them around."

"Ted, that's not nice. I'm not having talk like that."

"Bossy old bitch. Someone paid her out, I reckon."

She slapped a shirt of his on the table edge. "Ted. I mean it. That's enough."

He grinned and applied himself to his tea.

A hundred yards away at Saxhurst Court, Khalifa Abdurrahman held her son's head clear of the water as she soaped his body. Thronged round the baby bath, her daughters watched. After so much trouble, a boy; and did they notice what a difference it made to their father? Shahin, herself officially a woman now, was more occupied with her youngest sister who dabbled in the water as she held her up to see.

"Has anything been heard of Nanny Gray yet?" Nour asked.

"Not yet."

"I like it when she comes to see us."

"Only because she brings chocolate."

"No! No! I love Nanny Gray."

"If you have another baby, will she come and look after us again?"

"Who knows?" Khalifa said; but she thought: no, she won't. Never.

At the other end of the village, Emily

Playfair put down a saucer at the end of the row for Phoebe's cat Buffy Struggles, in his old place.

"I knew you'd not be with her long," she said. Her brown-spotted hand stroked along his back, which rose under the caress although he did not stop engulfing his supper.

At the Manor, Ken Cryer switched off the playback, rose from his swivel chair and stretched. He picked up the cigarette from the ashtray and wandered to the window.

"Rain starting up. Hope Jemmy gets in before it starts to really piss down. He's taken to that gruesome Mona Staveley. Hope she doesn't seduce him. God, isn't life here exciting? Think of it, a nanny goes missing. Take their minds off the orgy we're supposed to have had on Tuesday."

His profile was reflected against the yew tree: gaunt, clever, pale, a townsman's face, famous on album sleeves, posters, Smash Hits and in the spotlight.

"The fuzz will beetle up here again to make sure she wasn't coming to patch my suppurating needle tracks and I didn't slaughter her in a hallucinating frenzy."

A spiral of smoke came with the deeper, slightly Scots voice from the armchair.

"And did you?"

Ken suddenly pressed his face to the glass. "God, that *is* a police car coming up the drive."

"You should be more respectful."

Ken's nascent grin wiped. "Is Jemmy all right?" He hared for the door, fought the handle and hurtled off down the hall. His drummer, striding after, saw him open the front door on Jemmy and the local police sergeant.

"We found Miss Gray," Jemmy said. "She's dead. She's been dead quite a time, I think. They want me to show them where."

2

SUPERINTENDENT Bone oriented the map, and shifted round the table to survey it the right way up. He rubbed his eyes. Behind them still moved after-images of the night: the woods and the lamps, the flickering tapes striping the darkness, blowing leaves and light rain that hissed on the lamps; more driving through the night, on these country lanes where headlights dazzle; the pathologist, Foster, and his dislikeable job over the body, while Bone tried to take an intellectual interest.

The sergeant's pencil tapped the small coloured shapes.

"Here's where we were last night, sir. Amazing long walk, you'd say, for an old lady not always steady on her feet. Maybe it took her some time, though, wandering. It's in the Manor woods and there's the Manor. Our search hadn't reached that yet, it's two miles or so and we were concentrating on more likely areas at first, this stream near her house, those woods, the ponds. Miss Sidgwick, that's the niece, says the old lady used to like the Manor woods when she worked there. She'd looked after the boy there at the Manor three years back."

"Jemmy Cryer, one of the finders."

"The same. Quiet pair, him and his father. When Ken Cryer took the Manor we thought there'd be trouble, but they're a quiet pair, him and the boy, bar the occasional party that they always give us notice of, and that they had one on Hallowe'en. Cryer opened the Fair last Bank Holiday. He's generally liked. Keeps to himself, gets most supplies locally, which not everyone his sort might. It was along of Miss Gray having looked after the boy when he was younger, that Miss Sidwick's there now."

"The niece inheriting the post."

"You might say so. Last year Cryer was on a world tour, took the boy with him a lot of the time; she went to work there when they got back. Now this house, here, is the Arabs. Abdurrahman."

"Can I have that again?"

"Ab-du-ra-man, as near as you can get

it. Called the Abdus locally. Don't see much of them. In and out by car, pots of money, shop in London or Maidstone. Seven children, servants—not sure how many, they come and go all the time. Fairly westernized, they are, but occasionally you see one of them in one of those head-wraps, and they don't mix much."

Sergeant Cloke had a jovial fatness of face, sharp eyes and a small mean mouth, an uneasy combination. Bone knew about the short temper and the pretentious wife.

"Where does the other child live? Mona Staveley?"

"Here. Forge Cottage, Cross Lane. Father went off five years ago, last heard of in Southampton. Lodger, odd-job labourer, motor mechanic, has form for GBH, not a nice piece of work particularly when he's had a few. Bolshie. That girl's a very odd friend for the Cryer boy, not that he's any class but he gets asked to the local smart kids' parties. Couple of minders at the Manor, Jo Tench, Mel Rees, but they're law-abiding." He gave their impeccable histories. There was a pause.

Bone rasped his cheek.

"Enemies of the deceased."

Cloke straightened up. "Difficult, sir. She's got across a few people; fussy spinster, old-fashioned principles and none the worse for that. House-to-house may bring some word in. She came into money lately, Sir Gareth Herne over at Wiley, she'd been his nanny. Might be a lead in that, only there was no robbery."

"So far there's only the one suspicious circumstance," Bone said. He sighed. He felt short of oxygen. "I'll join Inspector Locker at Miss Gray's place."

"Hasn't he got your car, sir? I'll run you down there."

"No. I'd like to walk."

"It's the other end of the village."

Bone gave his fleeting smile and flipped the map. "I know." He walked out into the high street, musing at the dependence on transport that made the other end of the village seem a long walk away. His own grandfather had bored him with boasts of the amount of walking forced on him in childhood, deploring school buses and the motor car. The mileage that seemed walkable was shrinking by the decade.

The small town, or large village, sloped down a longish curving street, imaginatively called The Street. At the top were houses with gardens of all periods from timbered and skew mediaeval through Georgian beautifully proportioned boxes, gabled Victorian, neo-Georgian with the roofs too low and the windows too large, mock Tudor, and all sorts of honest and dishonest modern. Bone moved through a small crowd of early shoppers waiting for the bakery to open. Here, too, the parked cars began.

Bone crossed an entrance. PRIVATE ROAD. NO TURNING. SAXHURST COURT. Two dark, richly pretty little girls in breeches and lovat sweaters were leading a piebald pony out. Its feet, ter-clip-ter-tap, told of its unshod off-hind.

A warm smell beckoned as the bakery doors opened. Bone turned back, waited, and bought buns. Further down the street, a cheerful noise already issued from the radio and television shop, a record that might or might not be Ken Cryer's latest single from the album *Crying Shame*. Bone had heard it on the radio but could not be sure. Two small children watched a soundless cartoon beyond the glass.

Bone passed the Co-op, where a girl was putting trolleys out in a nesting rank. The Royal George; the greengrocer setting his display over half the pavement and arguing in a fractious bark with someone inside the shop; the Jobcentre, the butcher, chemist, Saxhurst Books, the outfitter, the Swan, estate agents, solicitors, the off-licence, bank, ironmonger, jeweller, newsagent, Saxhurst Antiques, Healthfood, Louise Gowns, a Chinese takeaway, chemist, and he was among houses once more. Opposite, as he came down, had been the Green, the Church, a duplicate row of shops, and the junction of the Maidstone road.

Here was Saxhurst Place, a William Morris success in old brick with a long swoop of tiles, among oak trees. Here, closer to the road and behind more vari-egated hedges crouched a row of cottages, with quite long gardens all the same. On a gatepost sat, heraldically, a calico cat with yellow eyes. Bone, as there were no pedestrians near, said "Prst?" and it rose to all fours, put up its tail, and extended a nose freakt with jet towards Bone's presented hand. It approved the hand and pushed its cheek along his knuckles.

Bone, scratching round the furry face and ears, liked the inconsequence of the black and orange markings. There were two more cats in the garden and, he suddenly observed, a woman at the window. She waved and nodded. Bone raised his hand in polite salute, hastily said a stern "Goodbye" to the cat, and strode away. Does there come an age in life, he wondered savagely, when one doesn't embarrass oneself over perfectly normal actions?

Here were the crossroads, the bridge, the lane. Houses at this corner had not decided which road to face, and Phoebe Gray's cottage was perched a little above the sunken lane, not facing the larger road. It was tile-hung, an old roof showing warped beams by the hills and valleys of its tiles. There was no sign of Bone's car, but a police motorbike stood in the garden.

Bone set out to cross to it, and a sudden blast of noise sent him leaping towards its gate as a second and, so to speak, profane motorbike came batting out of the lane and swerved past him, ridden by a beefy man in leathers with a peeling design on the wide back, and black ringlets flying out under his helmet.

Inspector Locker saw Bone coming up the brick path between lavender hedges, and had the door open. He was carrying his notebook. The door opened into a pleasant if dark sitting room, with an air of comfort despite its dark and chill. In the small kitchen behind, Locker unscrewed the coffee flask and poured Bone the cap full. Bone opened the bun bag between them on the table; he had been keeping his hands warm on it, and now he clasped them round the plastic mug and said "On your mark, get set, go."

"Here is the ashpan where Miss Sidgwick thought Miss Gray hit her head. That was the . . . yes, the thirty-first. Miss Sidgwick rang just now and she's coming here shortly to fetch a coat. She found Miss Gray sitting here confused, and helped her to bed, had to leave her because of a Hallowe'en party at the Manor where she had to help out, but Miss Gray told her that a friend, Mrs. Playfair, was coming in and that she herself felt better. Next day when she arrived, the old lady had gone. She then saw the blood on the ashpan. Here. Of course she cleaned it up."

"Damn," Bone said.

"Damn. But Dr. Foster says it's in the cracks, and he's got samples we took, together with a couple of the cork tiles. The stains on them may be scorches, cooking splashes, blood. They could be older bloodstains as she fell against that very place last spring."

"Have you seen Mrs. Playfair?"

"Should I go there now? I was waiting for you, sir. They're a bit stretched here, with it being weekend one of their blokes is in Calais, and one's away ill. PC Berryman's doing house-to-house along here. According to him, Mrs. Playfair's an eccentric."

"'Batty as a cricket' is the usual term," said a woman's voice in the garden. Bone clonked his cup down and opened the window wider. She stood on the brick path, in Hush Puppies, a tweed skirt and scarlet jumper. It was the cat owner, and she held a half-Persian tabby in her arms. "Wasn't *listening*," she went on. Alert light-blue eyes crinkled naughtily, "just overheard. One's name always interests, doesn't it? This is Buffy Struggles, Phoebe's cat. One of mine originally. I fetched him back when Carey told me Phoebe'd disappeared."

Locker had opened the door, and Mrs. Playfair headed for it and came in. She had silver-grey hair in a pageboy cut. Her hands, one with a big moss agate ring, clasped Buffy Struggles competently, though he was not true to his name and sprawled, placid, in her arms. Bone introduced himself and Locker.

"You can see," she said, as she sat down at the table and arranged the mass of fur loosely on her knee, "why the cat-flap had to be so big."

Bone had noticed the size of the hinged flap in the door. It was latched now. He had presupposed a small dog rather than a cat.

"Buffy's a neuter and they do so *grow*. Would it be all right for me to put him down?"

"It might be better if you didn't. We've not finished here."

"Well, he won't mind if I don't. The least exertion the better, that's his motto, a thorough Drone. And do finish your coffee; I've this moment breakfasted."

Locker obeyed, setting to work also on a bun.

"Were you a close friend of Miss Gray's?"

"Oh—I'm not sure anybody was, but if anybody was then it was I." She rearranged Buffy's bulk. "Phoebe could be very caustic, even with Carey though she was very fond of the girl. Certainly I was one of her friends and probably the closest, though only because I lived nearest. She didn't believe in me, of course. She'd say, 'Emily, you *should not* make up these stories, they will cause trouble.' Well, she's—she was right; they often have."

"Stories." He used the noncommittal, encouraging tone and she sent him one of her glittering sly glances. Her mouth twitched.

"I'm psychic. That's what made it difficult for her."

"It must be uncomfortable for you sometimes." Bone was not sceptical, he wasn't young enough any more. After Petra's death he had been sharply aware of her presence in the house for almost two weeks; then it had abruptly gone. He felt like asking Mrs. Playfair about Phoebe Gray's presence, but Locker inhibited him.

"Can I be useful? In plain questions, I mean?"

"Did you in fact see Miss Gray that Tuesday evening?"

"No, I didn't, and what's more I couldn't have done. Phoebe either was wandering in her mind, or she was simply trying to reassure Carey, because she *knew* I would be out. I was at Hastings all day."

"When did you in fact last see her?"

She looked at the table. Indeed, she stared at the buns with such concentration that Locker's hand, still clutching a biro, came out and pushed the bag slightly towards her. She stirred and said "I'm not sure, you see. There was Sunday morning. That's the twenty-ninth," she added to Locker, who had gone on with his quiet note-taking. "She went to Church, and she came to breakfast. An old arrangement. She wouldn't eat before Communion, but she used to feel a little ill by the time she reached home, and though she would set her breakfast ready, and have tea prepared in a Thermos, she found that she couldn't eat. She did not take *at all* kindly to my suggestion of taking a good swig of the wine, but she did agree to a breakfast ready waiting a few hundred yards nearer."

"Was that regular? Every Sunday?"

"No, only when there was early Communion here. First and third Sundays, and fifth when it so fell. She couldn't get to Rowden or Wiley in between. Mrs. Abdurrahman offered to send her car, but Phoebe didn't choose to accept."

"Mrs. Abdurrahman is—"

"Muslim. Yes. But thought a great deal of Phoebe. Visited her quite often, *with* presents, such as wine or a nice pie. Christmas hampers. All Fortnum's. I believe their servants all get some such token at one of their feasts, and she counted Nanny Gray as one of them still. Phoebe looked after Mrs. Abdab and the little girls when the last two children were born. Valued accordingly. I should think that she was a really excellent nurse. Though, this year, she was beginning to be shaky. Parkinson's, you know. Mrs. Abdab begged and begged her to go there, though, and in the end she went for the little boy's birth. I don't know that she had much real work to do, but she took charge, and she told me that Mrs. Ab needed company a good deal during her recovery. I really mustn't call her Mrs. Ab, much less Abdab, and I don't know why Abdurrahman should be harder to get one's tongue round than Fortescue or Smith-Whittaker. But 'Abdab' does so offer itself." She gave Bone a naughty glance. "It is *irresistible*. Well, the little Abdu girls all liked Nanny Gray. Yes. Sunday morning was the last time I saw her that I am sure of."

"What was breakfast on Sunday?"

"Kippers. Toast and marmalade, of course, and kippers. She was very fond of them, and I found that she had them herself for Sunday breakfast when she was alone, so I grilled them for us, and we would sit and have such a cosy . . ."

Emily stopped, and turned her head to stare fixedly out of the window. Her eyes had flooded. She fished a handkerchief from somewhere under the passive Buffy, dried her eyes and nose, and went on. "Then there was Monday evening. She used to walk up to the postbox with her letters, a great correspondence with her nurselings all over the world, more than a dozen of them, I should think. She went past my gate that evening."

"After dark?"

"Yes. You see that streetlight opposite my house doesn't make people clear. She didn't wave. Still it was obviously her and I don't know why I feel unsure." She placed a forefinger on the table. "I have to be careful, you know, because I do *see*. They used to be quite distinct in nature, the actual *seeing* and the physical seeing. Lately, I've been less sure. There's a case in point on the evening of last Sunday. I saw Gareth Herne with perfect clarity at this door here. Well, he's been dead some weeks, poor man. There was someone here, I suppose, and only a trick of the light made it look like Gareth. It didn't feel like Gareth. I met him here at

Phoebe's once or twice, he was a very amusing man. Then once he came to my house and asked if he could sit there for a while. He didn't feel well, he said, and it would worry Nanny; he looked very odd indeed, I think he was drugged. He watched the kittens for about an hour, thanked me, and went off. He said he knew I'd understand, and I felt flattered as one does. Poor man, I hope that dying of an overdose is either simply marvellous or quite painless."

Bone, with the knowledge that it might instead be quite horrific, moved on. "Had there been any arrangement for a meeting with Miss Gray later than that Sunday breakfast?"

"A rendezvous! An Assignation! No. Carey asked me that on Wednesday. Of course Phoebe told her there was, for the Tuesday evening. No such thing, I was at a little Hallowe'en party with some friends at Rowden after a day in Hastings, as Phoebe very well knew I would be. Typical of her to reassure Carey. She'd see that the girl was anxious to get away to that do at the Manor. Phoebe hated fuss, of course, and Carey does tend to. It must have been quite a party at the Manor; real rock-around-the-clock. The music went on till morning."

Buffy Struggles stretched, laid his head and a foreleg back on the table and there remained.

"He's not psychic," said Mrs. Playfair, a little sourly. "He's all stomach, that one. Doesn't miss her."

Bone was aware that she did miss Phoebe Gray, and here they were, a couple of strangers sitting all over her living room, a pair of official intruders. Emily Playfair's civilised social air made her seem unaffected by their presence. She stood up now, putting the cat across her shoulder. Bone, fetched to his feet, saw in the better light as she turned towards the door, that her face was drawn.

"It's best to talk about things as easily as one can," she said. "I know that. I'm old enough to have seen the deaths of friends. But, perhaps if you have more to ask me, if you find there's any way I might be useful, you'd come to my house. It's not right, here."

"Yes, I'm afraid it must be painful."

"There's been violence," she said. "Oh

no, I'm not one of those who can see past events. Not even sure I believe in them, though in reason I ought to do . . . no, it's like a foul taste in the mind, the violence. This was such a very peaceful house and Phoebe loved it. You know Gareth Herne gave it to her? It belonged to the family. When she talked of retiring, he asked if she'd like it. It's been a peaceful house, even when Carey lived here; an unquiet girl. But now I'd sooner go," and she moved towards the door. The cat, its paws over her shoulder as on a windowsill, eyed Bone indifferently.

"Can you just tell me," Bone made his voice gentle. "The person you mistook for Gareth Herne, that Sunday evening; did you recognise him?"

"No. He was there at her door for an instant and then gone. I wasn't even sure I'd seen him. If it was there, physically, it was a man and not a woman, but it hadn't a strong presence, such as Gareth always had."

"Thank you," he said, and opened the door.

She stopped outside and turned towards him. There was sunlight now, pale and cool. The blue eyes looked beyond him, then focused on his. She spoke in a different tone.

"It was the wrong wound, wasn't it?" she said and, not waiting for an answer, went away, her skirt brushing scent from the lavender. The flat face of Buffy Struggles regarded him in apparent irritation until she stepped down into the lane and was gone.

Bone shut the door.

"Well, sir, that's something to ask her about right off, wouldn't you say? What does she know about the wound?"

"We're not ready to talk about the wound yet," Bone said. "We wouldn't be here, I agree, if Foster hadn't found a very different kind of wound." He too gazed at the sharp corner of the ashpan jutting from the stove's base.

3

"WHAT Sergeant Cloke said about her, about Mrs. Playfair, was that she's a bit eerie." Locker, who could appear Plod to the life, was a connoisseur of character. "What do you reckon on her saying that?"

"M'm. A, she has some way of knowing about it from the doctor, from Berryman or Cloke, none of whom would talk about it, B, that she latched onto it from us by telepathy or C, it came to her from the ewigkeit."

"May one ask what that is when it's at home?"

"The wide blue yonder. In any case, would you say she's above putting it across us a bit?"

"No, sir. Only the way she said it looked convincing."

"And why shouldn't she be psychic? There remains the further possibility, which you won't have overlooked—" Locker turned a startled glance—"that she done it. Only the murderer is likely to know that the wound wasn't made with a sharp edge." Bone bent to glare at the inoffensive ashpan. Straightening up, he said, "Right. Berryman didn't find any nice blunt surfaces; he was looking at night. We've got daylight."

"Looking for a protuberance of round shallow superficies or for a blunt instrument," Locker confirmed. "I've been over the kitchen. It's all angles and corners and edges."

The cottage, two up and two-and-the-kitchen down, presented a surprising number of sharp corners. Upstairs, where Bone began, was dusty. The air felt still, undisturbed. Berryman's footprints lay on the floors.

In the back bedroom was no bed, only a polished space of floorboards with a blur of dust. The wardrobe held three identical uniform frocks, spotless and ironed, almost child-sized for a grown woman; a winter coat in a cleaner's bag, grey and navy skirts, and on the shelf a felt hat and a summer straw. The dressing table, small and empty, had no glass.

The smaller second room owned a neat

bed covered in brown chenille, a small table in front of a wall mirror, and some make-up in the table drawer; curlers, a box of tampons, an opened pack of tissues, safety pins and hairgrips. A hanging rail with a curtain round it held a fake fur coat like a despondent bear. A tall narrow chest of drawers harboured ribbed tights, assorted underwear, bright sweaters, woollen shirts and, in the lowest drawer, a couple of neatly folded uniform dresses, a petersham belt, and a laundry packet full of starched linen.

The floor sloped to the window, which looked out on the garden at the back. Bone's car was parked in a small hard stand at the end of the garden where Locker had backed it in.

Ducking, though he was not a tall man, Bone descended to the ground floor. Locker was in the little back room, which was crowded with a bed, whose foot and head boards presented only sharp corners, and which was neatly made with clean linen; a gate-legged table with its leaves down and a vase of moribund flowers on it—hothouse, gardener's flowers—and a gaunt oak dresser. Locker had been examining ornaments, which crowded the shelves. He shook his head.

The furniture missing upstairs was here: in the dresser, clothes, and on its surface and shelves, on the windowsill and table, on the corner whatnot, on the small bedside table, stood framed photographs, china souvenir toy-sized teacups and saucers glazed with "Swansea", "Scarborough" and "Torquay", or more classily Spode miniatures; a lopsided pincushion, child-made; a more skilful panholder, unused, embroidered "Nanny" in chainstitch; a piece of angular Derbyshire quartz; straw dolls, a family of wishbone mice in felt skirts and feather bonnets; framed drawings and amateur watercolours; wooden and alabaster eggs in a basket whose weave suggested childish hands; an expensive television set on its own neat trolley, its control on the bedside table. By the bed, with an angle lamp, a Bible and a Common Prayer soft with use, a Dorothy Sayers and *A Short Walk in the Hindu Kush*, was a personal stereo-cassette-radio, not much larger than a cigarette pack, with its wires and earplug speakers. On a shelf below, together with

A Time of Gifts and *Travels in West Africa* was a stack of cassettes: *Camelot*, *South Pacific*, the Beethoven *Sixth* and *Your Favourite Mozart*.

"No handy blunt corners, sir. I begin to concur with Berryman."

Bone did not distrust local constables or their power of observation. He merely required to be certain. "Outside, then, and—"

A knock fell on the outer door, which was then opened, and a young woman's voice enquired, "Can I come in?" Locker followed Bone into the sitting room.

She was pale, with light brown hair coming loose from the combs that held it either side. She wore a blue open-necked shirt, a brown woollen jacket and matching scarf, corduroy trousers, suede ankle-boots and woollen gloves she was pulling off. She said breathlessly, "I had to collect my coat. I rang up," and she looked round, hesitated, moved from foot to foot and then thrust out a hand to Bone. It was cold but firm, quite a large hand for a woman who was small but strong-looking.

Introducing himself and Locker, he said, "Miss Sidgwick."

"Yes. I met Inspector Locker at the Manor this morning early. It's a terrific blow. I still can't believe it. I mean, she did sometimes go away without telling me. I think she did it because she knew I was so concerned about her. Not to be cruel, I don't mean that, but to be independent, and she would do such dangerous things, like making her own jam, with all those boiling heavy pans, and then she's—she'd be likely to go off on what she called binges, little trips to some town or other, and I was so badly hoping she'd done that. It's been so awful."

"Won't you sit down?"

She sat on the old ottoman by the window. "I don't understand why you're still here. Didn't Auntie die of exposure?"

"We're afraid not."

"But that's terrible!" Her eyes opened to show white all round the brown irises. She sat with her mouth, too, ajar and then said, "Was it that bang on the head? Was it? She wouldn't let me look, let alone touch it."

"That seems to have been the cause of death."

"So why are you still here? If it was that?"

"Just enquiries, Miss Sidgwick."

"Oh yes, I see. I suppose you have to. They're out, at the Manor, until four, so I only have to have tea ready. I do teas only, except on Sim's day off. Would you like some tea or coffee? I could make you some. There should be powdered milk."

Bone was about to speak when she said, "And I suppose it shouldn't be touched. Though I did come in, after she'd gone, and I moved all sorts of things. Oh, won't you sit down?"

She evidently felt she was hostess.

"I still haven't realised. I mean, I did half think Auntie had gone on one of her excursions. Though it wasn't very likely, you know. Last spring she went on one, she told Emily but she didn't tell me. She called them binges. Of course she could afford to stay somewhere really nice now, so I hoped . . . Oh dear."

Breathless speech, the deep brown gaze that always seemed to be on something beyond, and the suggestion round the eyes that she had not slept, produced a curiously sexy aura round Carey Sidgwick.

"She used to go to b-and-b places or a cheap hotel, but she said it was an absolute holiday to be looked after for a bit. As if I wouldn't have done it, any time!"

"Suppose you start at the beginning."

She responded vaguely to his smile, but it was, after all, his official encouragement smile.

"The beginning? I suppose the beginning was Monday when she wasn't feeling well and stayed in bed. So I did her shopping for her. She got up later, just like her, because her letters were posted, when I looked. I was going to offer to take them because she always liked them to go on the Monday. It was the Tuesday when I saw they had gone. She was sitting there, where Inspector Locker is, when I came in, and she was vague. She said she'd tripped. She'd done it before, you see. She'd tripped over the cat. Buffy is very stupid, and she was shaky. She wouldn't discuss her health, and it was only when I'd been urging and urging her to see a doctor that she told me she had seen him some time ago and knew perfectly well

41

what was wrong with her, but she wouldn't tell me. Can you believe that? I'm a nurse, I'm qualified, but she wouldn't discuss her health with me at all. Well then, I left her to herself. She wouldn't even let me get her anything to eat or drink, though I thought I'd make her a flask of arrowroot, but no! Anyway, she told me that Mrs. Playfair was coming in the evening, and I knew Emily would look after her. Auntie was much less difficult with Emily than she was with me. She used to think I was only a girl, or something, too young. I don't think she ever took in that I was grown up. All the same, if it hadn't been for the party I wouldn't have left her. I wouldn't have. And Emily wasn't coming at all, she was away for the day and I didn't know. It was so *like* Auntie, making me go. I was anxious all evening—well, all night. The party went on until morning. There must have been an awful lot of drunken driving on the roads back to London. Some of them stayed, of course, even until afternoon next day. It was the sort of party people expect Ken to have, and he hardly ever does."

"When did you find Miss Gray was not here?"

"I suppose about ten o'clock. I didn't wake very early. It's very difficult to remember things exactly. She wasn't in. She hadn't made her bed, but I made it, and I found she'd had an accident—you know—so I changed the sheets and put them in the machine and tidied up a bit, waiting for her to come in. There was a little mark on the pillow, that worried me, you know, because with her not letting me look at her head, and her being shaky. I hoped she hadn't felt ill somewhere up in town. I went to Emily's, and that was when she told me she'd been away and not here and hadn't seen Auntie at all, so then I went round the shops, asking, and no one had seen her. I asked them not to tell her I'd been asking, because she so hates fuss. Then when I came back, I realised Buffy hadn't been fed. When I was in first, I thought he was putting it on, but this time I looked at his dish, and I fed him and then I looked round, and Auntie's little holdall that she called her binge bag was here, and her purse, so I panicked. I rushed to Emily and she went to the police with me."

"At what time on Tuesday did you last see her?"

"I was on my way to the Manor and a bit late, I'd been doing shopping. I suppose I didn't stay very long. Twelve thirty, about."

"Did you notice if she had made her bed on that day?"

Carey was startled. "Made her bed?" The question seemed to have thrown her. The brown glance wavered over the bedroom door. "No. I didn't *go* in there. Oh, it's so strange. And the police didn't seem very bothered when we went. Then after all they didn't find her." She put salt in the wound. "It was poor Jemmy. Though he seems more intrigued than traumatised."

"It's an unusual name, Jemmy." Bone wanted to lead to seeing the boy soon.

"Oh, that mother of his went all eighteenth-century and cute. Ken's father's name was James and he wanted the name, but she was set against it because of 'Jim' or 'Jimmy', which I believe she thought were common. So after

Ken wouldn't have Auberon or Lucius, she discovered 'Jem', and she thought that was cute because it meant 'jewel' too. I heard all this from the bodyguard."

"Would you tell Mr. Cryer that we'd like to talk to Jem this evening? About five, say?"

What she had come to collect was her fur coat. Locker wrote a receipt out and she signed it, and went away down the back garden to her car, which was drawn in awkwardly across the entrance to the stand. Bone watched her through Miss Gray's bedroom window. He said over his shoulder, "Impression?"

"People show things differently but, would you say she's that distressed about her aunt? Very likely it hasn't hit her yet. She's flustered but she's detached. Like watching herself being bereaved."

Bone swung round to listen with appreciation.

"She sounds to have been more timid with the old lady than you think she'd be; but I can see why Miss Gray got impatient."

"I suppose Miss Gray behaved like a Matron to her." Bone emerged from the bedroom and crossed to the bureau. The glass-fronted cupboard above it presented him with a ghostly reflection superimposed on plates. The face that approached was a bit cadaverous too. It would have been unfortunate, though more amusing, to have been a fat man called Bone; though in his daughter's case, when she became anorexic after her mother's death, it hadn't been amusing at all. Her best friend, Prudence, named with staggering inappropriateness, had always called her Charred Bone and now called her Skellington; Skelly for choice. Charlotte retaliated by naming her Grue. He had disliked the girl initially, but her friendship had sustained Charlotte and been a considerable factor in her physical recovery.

"Shortly," he said, "we'll see what the Swan does in the way of lunches."

The bureau provided a certain amount of interest. It was neat, as he would have expected. The prim asperity he associated with Miss Gray ensured that her papers were as much in order as her clothes. It was fortunate that she did not know, or it was to be hoped she did not, how messily she would lie on the earth.

Modern inventions did away with the need for reading blotting paper in the glass, though he had found this necessary in one case early in his career. Nanny Gray used a ballpoint pen, an expensive one kept in its box. She used three sizes of envelope, in their pigeonhole—long and short manila, large squarish white. Her writing paper was a plain block, white. Next to the envelopes' pigeonhole were maps, local large-scale ones marked along the footpaths with pen lines. Those walks went for quite a distance round the countryside and included the Manor woods where she had been found. The third pigeonhole held postcards and letter-cards, the fourth was full of receipts for rates, gas, electricity, water, newspapers, telephone and milk delivery.

The drawer beneath yielded to Bone's long fingers a cheque book, with stubs meticulously filled in and each entry subtracted from a total; a television licence, a telephone dialling-code booklet, a small mail-order catalogue of the selective kind, a box of National Trust notelets half used, and a large heavy manila envelope: Phoebe Janet Gray. WILL. Photocopy. Original at Bank.

Bone was always aware of his authorised prying. After so long it still gave him a sense of the furtive, so that if interrupted he had the impulse to hide what he looked at. He opened the Will distastedly.

Phoebe Janet Gray had left small bequests to Emily Playfair, to a nurses' fund and to an animal welfare association. She left named articles, "my Joseph Farquharson snow scene", "my stump-work box" to the said Emily Playfair and others, a paintbox, a footstool, a japanned tea caddy, a millefiore paperweight, a box of puzzles, a silver pencil, to various children; or so they must be because Bone knew two of the names, James Cryer, Mona Staveley, and he supposed that Shahin Abdurrahman was one of the children from Saxhurst Court. The residue after duties, funeral expenses and "any just debts" was left outright to Carey Susan Sidgwick. The ritual provision "if she survive me for thirty days" made Bone grimace. Carey and Mrs. Playfair might expect to survive for what was left of the thirty days. There might be some doubt as to exactly when that period commenced.

Not so very many hours ago, on the night between October and November, the Manor's ancient timbers vibrated to the amplified thud, clash, swoop and shimmer of rock. The dining room had been cleared and was awash with dancers, but there was dancing anywhere, and a species of it in such bedrooms as were not locked. On the steps of the dining room, a reveller sagged suddenly against an oaken upright. The sight of that inland sea of bobbing heads, which the disco lighting made alternately recede, expand and vanish, finished him. Presently he slid down to the floor where he proved immediately to be a hazard to shipping and was dragged aside into the hall.

"He'll be all right there."

"What?"

"He'll be—all—right—THERE."

"Yeh." Things've only just about got started, they yelled. Where'd he get so pissed?—Been mixing it. Look at those pupils. Ugh. Yeugh. Mind your shoes.

A crack of laughter came from the

slighter of the two guests and he scrambled back out of range, fell against the house staff and said "There's an early casualty down there."

"Leave him to me, sir."

"Don't know how he managed not to puke on that pretty satin. God! He has, though! Sooner you to cope than me."

"That's all right, sir. We'll just pop it in the machine and him in a bed."

They picked their way past the sprawled figure and joined the dancers. The minder picked up the white figure, swung a chair over the mess on the floor to prevent anyone's treading in it, and carried the inert form away.

4

THE Swan provided a choice: pizza, lamb curry, sausage and mash. This seemed to Bone the least unattractive, but Locker chose curry. Luckily the ochreous dollop in a frill of rice pleased him, while Bone's sausages proved to be meaty, the mash made of real potatoes with a happy irregularity of texture, and the green beans tasted convincing. The sweet restored him to cynicism. It was called "trifle" and made of sturdy jelly, sodden sponge and insipid custard. A rosette of watery cream failed to support a small blob of violent red jam.

Coffee came hot, strong, like a beautiful woman with a sharp tongue. Locker asked to have his flask filled with more of the same. The waitress drew her mouth together, said "That great flask'd empty the pot. I'll get you some fresh made."

"Mind it's as good as this," Locker said, saluting her with his cup. She gave a tilt of her hip at him as she turned away, and

51

he grinned. His grin stayed as he watched her go. He sighed and turned to Bone.

"So, this afternoon?"

"Mona Staveley for starters."

Cross Lane, an unmade side lane behind the church, descended ruggedly. Locker viewed its surface and prudently parked at the top. They schussed down the loose surface, their feet arrested by lumps of hard core that had been dumped to fill a previous set of potholes. A new set was steadily forming between.

A brick yard, clean-swept and glowing red except for an oil patch beneath a gleaming motorbike near one wall, sported washing they had to duck. There was a pushchair with a plastic bag of washing perched on it. A roar of "Come on in" answered their knock.

The bike's owner, long dark curls and greying-out black T-shirt, bulked at the table, knife and fork upright, over baked beans and bacon, with squares of white bread lavishly buttered. A brown tea cosy sagged comfortably near his right elbow, flanked by a milk carton. A mug of tea the shape, and respectably near the size, of a chamber pot steamed by his plate.

He regarded them affably. In the corner by the cooker, a pale shadow in jeans and sweater lurked.

"What can I do for you? It's the fuzz, ennit?"

The pale shadow whipped out of the far door and up the stairs. The man gestured at the ceiling with his knife. "She thinks you're after her. She's a kelptomaniac."

Bone's rogue imagination supplied him with visions of wild bands of seaweed thieves. He said civilly, "We would like a word with her. Is Mrs. Staveley in?"

"Ner. She's at the Swan, dinner time. You want her, she'll be back at half two."

Bone swung his arm to see the time. It was after two; he said, "Can Mona be persuaded that we're not after her for any misdeeds?"

"I could tell her all right. As to if she'll believe me, that's another thing. And you're the bloke nearly had me off my bike at Mouse Corner, right?"

"You're the bloke nearly ran me down at Mouse Corner."

A bean-bedecked smile lit Larkin's face.

He waved a fork. As a man with form, he had surprisingly little animosity to the Force.

"That's right. You want me to fetch Frankenstein's Daughter down?"

"We'd rather wait until her mother is present."

"Won't be long. Take the weight off your plates."

"Thanks." Bone chose a chair at the table. Locker effaced himself on the sofa, which resembled a comfortably fat woman who has abandoned her corsets with relief.

"I'd like to ask you a few things too."

"Call my lawyer, shall I? I'm easy, if you don't mind me eating. I got a job s'afternoon."

"On Saturday?"

"It's all money. Bloke's car breaks down, garage doesn't work Saturdays, he don't want to spend fifty nicker getting the twenty-four-hour Maidstone lot."

"You do gardening too."

Larkin pulled a card from the breast pocket of the jacket hanging on his chair and pushed it across. "Edward Larkin. Auto mechanic. Electrical work. Handyman. c/o Staveley, Cross Lane,

Saxhurst," and a phone number. Bone liked its lack of pretension. He gave it back. Ted was gleaning tomato sauce with a piece of bread.

"You did some digging for Miss Gray in the summer?"

"Carrot trench. Yeh. Used to do all that herself. Stood over me, the old besom. She always knew better than anyone. Asked me later to dig over a grass patch but I said she could keep it. She'd have had me tying feeders on the earthworms. And after the way she treated our Mona—well, the kid helps herself, we all know about it. Now Cloke and Berryman know about it, ta very much Nanny. All the kid does is take a comic off Simmonds—"

"The stationers. Yes."

"Big deal, ennit? A comic. So Nanny tells May Simmonds and then what but a battleaxe of a WPC comes and scares Mona to death. Name of Fredricks, face like a space invader. Over a comic! And then what comes out, eh? Nanny had put Mona over her knee for helping herself to cash what she'd left about. There it was, laying on the dresser, what she expect? Mona don't go looking for money and she don't help herself from handbags. Never. It was laying there. Could've had her to court for assault, hitting the kid, and so I told her."

Bone surveyed the mutually incomprehensible sets of moral values, and shook his head.

"Think we couldn't?" Larkin demanded.

"I was thinking," Bone said frankly, "that it's hard to understand people."

Larkin took this as he had hoped, and relaxed. "June said to her—Mona's mother, right, June—she said to her, you lock up money properly like you should and you won't have no trouble. Well, that old witch is gone. Too bad. I'm not pretending I'm sorry. Why Mona spent time there at her place I'll never know."

"You're fond of the child."

"She as good as got no father. He has his bint in Southampton, good for him, but I'm here with June. I'm not hiding anything. When he first left her he used to turn up and get money off of her." Ted's hand jarred flat on the table. "Not after I started lodging here."

He finished his plateful and pushed it

away, reached for the jam jar and set to work on what remained of the bread and butter.

"Mona's funny," a forefinger whirled briefly at his temple, "but she's all right. Yes, you could say I'm fond of her. We get on."

He pointed his knife suddenly at Bone, and darkened.

"But I never touched that old bag on her account. Words we had, I don't deny. She'd no call to be so mean to the kid, she wasn't so perfect herself with her drinking and that, but I never touched her. I don't hit old women. Don't you think it."

Passing up the urge to say "How old does a woman have to be for you not to hit her?" Bone said, "Surely nannies only drink tea? What's that about her drinking?"

"Leave it out! With her falling over in the shops, and that shake she had in the hands, let alone the bottle in the ashbin, and the bottle in the cupboard, and it wasn't sherry either. Gordon's."

"When did you see that?"

Ted grinned, pushing the empty bread plate away. "Cupboard was open when I knocked at the door. She totters off to get her garden hat and there's the Gordon's, and another in the bin when I empty her kitchen rubbish for her."

Bone was not of the opinion that two gin bottles stood evidence of serious drinking. Ted knew nothing of the Parkinson's. He himself in his early years had made a mistake that had nearly killed a man he'd diagnosed as drunk; he had locked him up, and then the man's wife rang the station to have him traced, because she'd found the tablets that he always had to have with him.

"Most kids were leery of the old bag, because she didn't mind who she told off. They made fun of her too. But one or two kids really liked her, and Mona kept going there. That's how she met up with Jem Cryer."

For the last few minutes there had been a susurrant noise on the stairs, and the crack of the stair door now darkened. Bone hoped the child was being reassured by the conversation, harmless to her and not aggressive towards Ted.

"You know the Cryers; worked at the Manor."

"Yeh, when they first came. Garden was a mess, old Smithy that looks after it needed a hand. He's all right, Cryer. Used to come out with beer every so often, paid reasonable too. Never said much, but he never came on the star; wheeled the barrow to the compost a couple of times, things like that."

"What about his music?"

"It's all right. Some of it's got a good beat. Bit arty."

The stair door had definitely opened. Bone kept his eyes from it and said, "Do you know the woods round there?"

"Yeh. Used to go courting there when the house was empty. Don't know where-abouts old Nanny was found. Mona's no good at telling where it was. Are you, Mone?"

"No," breathed Mona on the stairs.

"Do you drive a van?" Bone asked him.

"If anyone wants a van driven. Don't own one. That's my transport out there."

"And it wasn't Miss Gray who bruised your chin."

Ted's appreciation showed in a sidelong glance and a sucking of the teeth. "Ner. Had this off Bill Wheatley in the George.

Bit of a disagreement a week ago or more."

"How was Bill Wheatley?"

"Ah well, they broke it up, didn't they. Wouldn't let him come back in."

"Win your fights, do you?"

"Mostly. Got laid out by Cryer's minder, when they first come here. I didn't know him then. Mel Rees. He's all right."

Mona had emerged. Behind Ted's wide back she came softly and leant there, so that he seemed to be wearing a barn owl on his shoulder.

Mona thought the policeman had a face all corners, pale brown but his hair paler still so you could think he was quite old, but he did not have many lines except round his eyes. Ted was not angry with him so he must be safe.

"We're trying to establish the last time Miss Gray was seen. When did you last see her?"

Ted thought. She heard his chin all gritty on his collar as he chewed his cheek. "Be that Monday, I should reckon. Evening, getting dark. She was at her gate going in as I went by. Gave her a shout but she didn't answer."

"Was that usual?"

"She was a bit lahdidah about yer shouting in the street. Reckon she useter think I was taking the mickey when I was only being friendly. Had her moods too, the old cat."

Mona spluttered.

"Pack it in, Mone. Don't need my neck washed."

She took the tea towel he had used to get his dinner from the oven, and wiped his neck with it. That made him laugh and, pleased, she rubbed harder but he stopped her with a backward slap to the leg.

"You didn't see Miss Gray after that time on the Monday?"

"Ner."

"I did," Mona said. Monday was half term, home from school, memorable. "I saw her in the morning. She was dead."

"Yeah," Ted said, and she saw his cheek go fat as he winked at the policeman.

"I did see her, I did." It made her feel important.

He half-turned his head. "How'd you know she was dead, then? She tell you so?"

"Cos her hand was stiff like wood." She now had both policemen's attention, even the writing one on the settee had looked at her. "Nanny's whole arm wouldn't move."

Her mother's feet stamped up the steps, clicked across the yard, and stopped in the doorway.

"Oh yes?" she said. "What do you want?"

The policemen stood up, and the fair one said, "Mrs. Staveley. We met at the Swan," and they talked and all Mona's story was ignored. True, the thin fair one was thinking about it because he glanced at her sometimes; and after more useless talk he said again, "You saw Miss Gray in her house, Mona?" He wasn't stupid. He remembered.

"Yes. All stiff."

Mum laughed. "She's thinking of her Nan. Getting mixed up as usual. Mona does, mister. You know . . ." and she raised her eyebrows the way she did, that made people turn all sugar-soft to Mona or else talk to her loud and slow as if she were deaf. "She gets mixed up about what she sees. What she makes up, too. She's got such an imagination! Bad enough finding Nanny Gray in the woods, you'd think, without making out she'd found her in her house too. No, she's mixed up Nanny, what Miss Gray said she could call her, and her own Nan, and she wasn't supposed to see *her* when she was dead, either, but Mona gets in everywhere, don't you, love? I came in the room where the coffin was and well! there was Mona right by the side of it. Now Mona: be sensible like you can be. The policeman wants to know about you finding poor Miss Gray in the woods. You tell him."

Mona saw her other story blow away. Resigned, she settled for the woods. "Me and Jem and Prices, it was Prices found her first."

"Prices," said the fair policeman.

"He's Jem's dog. He got him when they came back from on tour. Jem went round the world with his dad."

"The dog found Miss Gray."

"T'wasn't Miss Gray." Mona knew the police had to have the exact truth, when it was possible to tell it. "It was her body.

She'd been dead, and things had eaten her a bit. Jem said after, it'd be foxes and weasels."

"You didn't tell me that!" Mum was shrill.

"She told me," and Ted put an arm round her, which he didn't often; and reassured by his strong comforting smell of sweat and oil, she peered doubtfully at her mother. Ted said, "Go on. You're doing all right."

"It was that awful we looked and looked. Then when the leaves came off her face we couldn't look no more. It was like a horror movie. Me and Jem talked about it. He said we had to tell the police, so we came up through the woods to the corner where the phone is but there was someone in the box talking and talking and when Jem opened the door to explain this man just swore and shut the door again, and so we went up to the station."

"Why they didn't go straight and phone from the Manor I don't know," Mum said. "Kids, they don't think."

Jem had said that if they went to the Manor, to phone, other people would take over, and instead they had gone all the way

64

to the station and it had felt marvellous marching in and saying over the counter, "We found Miss Gray." Jem had said it but she'd joined in. It was better than any phoning.

"What was the last time you saw Miss Gray before that?" the copper asked. He had a nice voice that wasn't bothered.

Mona hesitated. Mum would jump down her throat if she said about Nanny being dead in bed, but she ought to say it because she'd told them that already. She wasn't supposed to see things Mum didn't like, either. Nan's arm had been solid. She'd cried and been sick after and Mum had said it'd teach her not to go creeping in where she shouldn't go.

"Go on, Mone. Did you see her in the house? In the street?" Ted's arm gave her a bit of a shake.

"Don't know," she said, relieved at finding a safe way out. There couldn't be trouble if you didn't know. If they went on asking, you just started crying and they would stop. The copper didn't ask any more, though.

"Something a bit wrong with that kid,"

Locker said as they got into the car again. "I mean, she really liked all that stuff she was telling us."

Bone massaged his palms on the wheel. "She hasn't learnt to be shocked yet, though her mother's working on it. Still a bit more honest than most children her age, who've got ideas on what you're supposed to feel."

"What d'you reckon on her saw-Nanny-dead story?"

"It doesn't fit the facts so far known. Her mother's likely to be right. Let's file it for the present. Larkin, now. He looks like an oaf but he's sparking on all cylinders. Let's get back," and he turned the ignition, "and see if any info's come through."

In the incident room, co-opted from the Citizens' Advice Bureau near the station, Bone started to take off his coat and then found that the place was colder than outdoors. WPC Fredricks said "Storage heater doesn't work, sir. I'm told it's the cuts. We're getting a heater soon. Sorry about it."

She handed him her collation. Pathology, in Dr. Foster's factual account of the depredations of wildlife and of time, was only more detailed than Mona's account and included areas she had not seen. The first estimate about the wound was now conclusive, detailed examination proving it was the result of contact with an object of round shallow superficies, fracturing the posterior parietal bones and rupturing the dura mater causing haemorrhage and resulting pressure . . . Locomotion would be possible for a limited time . . . Foster was noncommittal to the point of hedging about the estimated time of death. He put it at up to a week, giving mention of damp, depredations and temperatures. There were unsatisfactory contradictions and he was making further examination. She had recently eaten kippers, and death had occurred not long after a meal that included tomatoes, whose indestructible seeds had not yet left the upper abdominal cavity.

Bone and Locker set off for the Manor in silence and a second-hand aura of decay.

Towards the end of the small street, Bone noticed a call box, and drew up by it. "Meant to call Charlotte from the station." He sorted change from his pocket. "Shan't be a moment, Steve."

Locker amiably said, "Give her my love, sir."

The call box, smelling of forty years of cigarettes, aimless frustration, and dust, refused even a dialling tone, and he emerged frowning. He hadn't called from the Swan, thinking he would be at the station before long; she might be, though not anxious, feeling his neglect.

A penetrating soprano hailed from across the road.

"Mr. Bone!"

Mrs. Playfair trotted down her garden path towards the gate.

"It's been out of order for days. They say it has water in the parts underground. You can telephone from here though." She swept a hand towards her house. "If it's official business—" she paused as a van passed along the road between them "—I shall stay out in the garden and you'll be completely private."

He crossed the road. Locker, seeing this, extracted himself from the car and followed.

"Thank you, Mrs. Playfair. The fact is,

I try to telephone my daughter if I'm away for long when she's at home alone."

Mrs. Playfair had opened the gate and stood back, beaming.

She shut Bone into a small room overlooking the crowded greenery of a little back garden. There was a desk, most of its surface taken up by a sprawled, rusty-black fur whose convolutions were at first indecipherable. Bone edged the telephone free of it and a shiver twitched round the periphery. His dialling made the fur clench tighter and a tail briefly thrashed. By the time he got through, the cat had relaxed again. Charlotte's voice came, soft and deliberate, giving the number.

"Hallo, Cha."

"Daddy."

"I don't expect to be late tonight. Six or half past. How has the day been?"

"Not bad." She did not like the phone. "No bad events." She avoided words starting with "th" and avoided it even in "nothing".

"Finished the homework?"

"Mostly. Daddy, you will—" she paused and he waited. "You will be fer-ree on Friday?"

"I've got the date written down and underlined and so on, and I'm booked off duty and they all know it's your school play. I've done all I can to be sure I'll be there."

"Hope you can make it."

"I mean to. Nice to hear you, love."

She made a kiss noise, he made one; they rang off.

He stood with his hand on the phone. He was feeling haunted again. Nanny Gray's had been the second death from head injury he'd had to investigate since The Accident. Everyone got such cases. It wasn't a special fate, only luck. Charlotte's speech centres were getting back into order in their own good time.

He put money for the call by the telephone, and on impulse laid his hand lightly on the centre of the black fur and massaged. After a surprised chirrup, the cat stretched a little and rolled over into a position not unlike a croissant, exposing its underside to his caress. It was enormous, probable a neuter male. He watched the paws for any tendency to fold up and claw.

Hearing the chink of cups, and Locker and Mrs. Playfair in the kitchen, he muttered "So long, cat," and withdrew. Locker was carrying a tray into the front room.

The big low room had no ceiling except plaster between the beams. The brick floor, covered here and there with rugs, glowed. There were two small chintz sofas, a couple of wicker armchairs, some wooden stools and a profusion of tables.

Mrs. Playfair poured tea into large bulbous cups. The cosy was velvet patchwork. She dispensed Dundee cake with a liberal hand, and sat back evidently pleased at giving hospitality. Some eyes have a twinkle in them; it is supposedly an Irish property, but there is not a monopoly and Mrs. Playfair's eyes had it.

"Your daughter is quite all—?"

She stopped there, turned towards Bone, her hand suspended near her cup; she was staring at the floor, at nothing he could see. She picked up her cup and said, "Your daughter has trouble with speaking."

Bone's eyebrow enquired of Locker, who shook his head. No, of course Steve would not have discussed it. Bone said,

"Yes. Since an accident a—a couple of years ago."

"Well," she said, reaching over to unhook a cat's claws from the table edge as it made an effort towards the cake, "I could have heard it from someone but I *think* I saw it. She's very thin?"

"Yes."

Emily Playfair shook her head slightly, as if to clear it, and took up her plate.

"Do you frequently see such things?" Bone was diffident. He had not come across anyone in this line who convinced him until now. His general attitude might be influenced by a recent case in East Anglia where a clairvoyant had located a missing boy; but clairvoyants had been proved at fault too. He felt it was an art, not a science; a fallible gift depending on a dozen interacting elements.

"Frequently? . . . no, sometimes they come in a rush. It may be months that I've not had an inkling. Probably it depends on my state of mind. I'd a friend who used to prate about psychic energies, and I think she was right, though she was such a tiresome woman that I see as little of her as I can now. It may at present be the shock of poor Phoebe's death. And then, some sensitives say it depends on what they eat." Mrs. Playfair's eyes crinkled. "Remember Madame Arcati and the red meat? But I'm not a medium. The dead don't talk to me. They never have and I hope they never do. I'd be very uncomfortable. No, I see things, that's all. I'm not a seventh child. But I don't talk about it much, I don't like to. It's a chance thing."

She might have caught Bone's line of thought.

"Another piece of cake, Mr. Locker? Oh do."

"Thank you."

He envied Locker. The cake was good but the piece he had got overfaced him. At this moment a slim glossy cat in tasteful shades of black and ginger sprang lightly onto his lap and gave his plate a professional stare.

"Arletty," Mrs. Playfair introduced. "She has hollow legs. Watch your cake."

"Is she allowed it?"

Mrs. Playfair rose to take the teapot for a refill. "If it did her harm, the amount she's eaten in her life would have done her in long ago. She'll eat anything. Anything at all."

Bone broke a corner of cake and held it idly in his palm; Arletty whiskered it, tilted her head and neatly lifted the piece, ingested it, and looked up in his face sweetly. As Mrs. Playfair returned, Locker asked, "How many cats do you have?"

"Counting kittens too, fifteen." She refilled Bone's cup and he gratefully drank. As he leant forward, Arletty's slender glove came over and hooked a large piece of cake into range. She picked it from his plate and jumped down with it, and he felt her working it over next to his ankle. Mrs. Playfair counted.

"There's Phoeb's Buffy Struggles, of course, and his full brother Rockefeller. Their sister's one of the two breeding queens and she's nursing five this time. She's Daisy. There's Arletty and there's Mameluke, who was I think in the study where you telephoned. There's Big Dorrit. Started as Little Dorrit, but a local tom soon changed all that. She's the other mother. She has four young cats, at present named Pringle, Hottentot, Gobstopper and Miss Flite."

Locker mused on this information. Bone ate what was left of his cake.

"People unload cats on me. Sometimes people take or buy cats from me. I sell often, but I give them if I think it's to a good home. Phoebe fell in love with Buffy when he was no bigger than—" she stood up and pattered into the next room, whence she emerged, shutting the door with adroit foot, carrying two pale handfuls. She gave one to each man. Bone received swansdown in which minute fishbones made an armature. There were amazing blue eyes.

"Half chinchilla," she said, "and favouring the sire." She compassionately took Locker's palmful of cloud away. Bone's kitten writhed vaguely. He put it on its back and scratched its stomach, and for a moment had it soothed, caught its attention. Then, writing more purposefully, in several directions, it turned over and he gave it back to Emily. She went off with them, to placate the anxiety audible next door. She said as she came back, "The Abdurrahmans have two of her last litter. The little girls wanted them after having Buffy in the house. I said they were very expensive, but they turned up next morning with a cheque from Mr. Abdu."

"Buffy was in their house?"

"When Phoeb went there. She'd have left him with me but Mrs. Abdab couldn't be too hospitable. Since then, too, nothing has been too good for Nanny Gray."

Another of those sparkling sharp glances.

"She gave me an odd impression, did Mrs. Abdab."

He used his inviting silence. This shrewd woman, by no means deficient in marbles, had made a decision to talk.

"I felt she wanted to placate Phoebe, to keep her sweet. I asked Phoeb why, teased her about it. I'm an inquisitive old bat. She told me that people coming out of anaesthetic could be very talkative, and that Mrs. Abdab (but Phoebe would never have called her that) thought she'd said too much. Phoebe could not convince her that anything she'd said was nonsense, that she'd paid no attention."

Arletty had got upon Locker's knee, and he had put her down. Mrs. Playfair saw her about to spring up again, and swooped, taking her on her own lap.

"I do *not* suppose, or mean to suggest, that I think Mrs. A did Phoebe any harm, but suppose her husband, or one of those Lawrence-of-Arabia types they keep up there, thought that Phoebe was a threat? I can't think it totally impossible that one of them could have done it. I am completely at a loss to think of anyone else who would."

She folded the cat up on her lap. Arletty's ears showed that she was not quite pleased, but she stayed for the moment under the ringed hands.

"Whereas Carey Sidgwick stands to gain quite a lot of money if Phoebe does leave as much to her as she told me she would, I *do* think it unlikely that Carey would."

Bone tried a little misleading tactic. "You don't think that Miss Gray became dizzy, as she was apt to do, and fell? And got up and wandered out?"

"No," she said. "There was violence, and the wrong wound. You know you asked me when I last saw Phoebe? I saw her in my mind this morning just after I'd left you. I seemed to be back in her cottage. I saw her struck down, but who did it I didn't see, there was such a mist

77

of anger; only something shone like a cat's eye, coming down on her. I don't know if it was man or woman—I can never look, I can only see. I saw Phoebe's face as she fell."

This time she made no attempt to conceal the tears, just wiped them away in an almost business-like fashion. Arletty, as if objecting to the emotion, slapped her tail against Emily's thigh.

Emily then sat up, straightening her back, and offered a plate to Locker. Bone, imitating her attitude and to give her a chance to recover, asked a neutral question.

"Where else has Miss Gray worked round here?"

"Everywhere!" The small hand flew out. "Well, first she spent years with the Hernes over at Herne Hall. Gareth, the elder boy, was delicate, and Lady Herne, that's his mother, not the present one, quite despaired of his life more than once, but Phoebe nursed him through. Then there was the younger boy Valentine; they're both highly strung, I believe. Lady Herne died soon after he was born, and Phoebe stayed as something like mother for a good many years. Gareth gave her that little house. The Hernes used to own a good deal of property round here but it's all been sold off. Gareth sold most things that weren't entailed."

"Was the family short of money?"

"Gareth couldn't have been. Phoebe was very startled by the amount of money he left her. It almost distressed her. I said, 'Phoeb, it can sit in the bank and you can spoil yourself a bit. You are not obliged to do anything with it but that.' She said she could do some useful things with it, and of course I agreed. She meant charities. I suppose there was tax on it, death duties, I don't know, but it still seems to have been a huge amount. I'm not sure the sale of property wasn't part of the quarrel between Gareth and his brother. Valentine's main pastime was disapproving loudly of his brother, who to do him justice gave plenty of cause. Well then, Phoebe nannied some boys in the north for a while, and then the Cryer boy when his mother left when they first came here, that would be five years ago. Then the Abdabs, twice, for the little girl and then the son."

79

"I see. Miss Sidgwick seems to have inherited the Cryer post."

"Though not really *nanny*, more as housekeeper. There's a cook, and the bodyguards, and sometimes guests, and very occasional parties like this week's when there's quite a lot of work."

"They don't use outside caterers?"

"I really don't know. Phoebe said that Carey always spoke as if she had to do all the cooking herself and the clearing up too, but there was always help for that. I know they had extra heavies to keep order."

"Heavies," Bone said, appreciating the small incongruity of the word on Emily Playfair's lips.

"We're very well supplied with them around here. Some of the Abdu servants are bodyguards. There are the two at the Manor, and, as I said, more when they entertain. Phoebe made very good friends with a seven foot high black man. He was here again this week, he passed here with the car that morning. I'm a great sitter at windows, Mr. Bone. When I was a girl we were taught that peering out of windows was as vulgar as shouting in the street. We were hedged about with dozens of little rules."

"Was there much local interest in the party?"

"Ken Cryer buys locally, so people do chat about it. The Abdabs of course shop in London because of their religion." She craned slightly to see the road, so Bone and Locker looked too. Miss Sidgwick was driving slowly by in the wake of a farm tractor.

"It's time I was on my way," said Bone. "Thank you for the refreshing tea."

"And useful chat, I hope," said Emily Playfair.

"And most useful chat," Bone smiled. Emily, surprised at what the smile did to that cautious, closed face, and at what it did to her, pressed his arm lightly and tapped it thrice, a friendly message in her own Morse: D, for dear man, don't worry.

5

THE Manor had an entryphone at the gate, which was well up the private drive from the road. Up to that point, the drive had been wall to wall hard core, over which Locker drove with care. Bone thought it was well devised to discourage both pedestrians intent on being silly with the entryphone, or a fast run at the gates. Once through the gates, which opened like magic, the drive ran smooth between rough-cut lawns among oaks and chestnuts.

The Manor lifted Bone's heart. It was a Tudor collection of tan beams, red herringbone brick, cream plaster and small mullioned windows, with long slopes of roof pulled low. It had settled into the ground, all at different heights and varied angles, with an inconsequence that suggested some sixteenth-century family adding rooms as they felt the need for them. Though quite a large house, it was no mansion.

Carey Sidgwick at the door was a brisk competent figure in blue trousers and sweater. She was much the same build as her aunt but stockier. The hairstyle, with its centre parting and two combs holding the light brown hair back from her face, did nothing for her.

"Jem is just home," she said. At close quarters, her manner combined the nervous with graciousness, welcoming guests but not quite as hostess. She led the way through the small stone-flagged, panelled hall, down steps to a brick-floored passage with a row of hooks where hung a man-sized black duffel coat, a boy-sized black duffel coat, various anoraks, and a long Inverness cape with a lining of mustard tartan so horrible that it must be genuine.

The room she led them to was floored with wide pale boards, and smelt of woodsmoke. It was small, with an inoffensively fake brick chimneypiece where woodash was piled in the hearth, and a three-seater sofa and two easy chairs in brown tweed scuffed on the arms. The windows and a French door gave onto the paved terrace, and opposite the windows, bookshelves rose to the ceiling.

"Do sit down. I'll hurry Jem." She left them.

Locker looked at the garden, Bone at the books. It was an untidy collection, with a great many paperbacks and only a couple of matched sets in hardback. He had quite expected Deighton, le Carré, Freeling; Asimov and Simak were not unexpected. Dickens, though it resembled a presentation set, showed some handling. Jung he had not expected at all, which gladdened him. Dorothy Dunnett, both Lymond and *Dolly*; Fraser, *The Dying God*. Ed McBain, Dick Francis, yes, but *With Mystics and Magicians in Tibet*? What was the man like who had congregated this little lot?

The door opened. In came a tea trolley —Bone sighed—and Carey Sidgwick. The boy pattered after and shut the door. His rather wide grey eyes took in Locker and turned to Bone, and he came forward with his hand out. Thin, with tousled mousefair hair, in cavalry twill trousers and a baggy Breton jersey in rust and black, he gave a hand to all corners, but with a firm grip. Full marks, too, for spotting the man in charge. How did it show, Bone wondered?

Carey opened up the trolley's leaves with a sharp jerk. The boy said, "Do please sit down," and picked up a plate of sandwiches and one of cake, while Carey poured tea. "Sugar? Milk?" She offered cups and plates. Locker chose an armchair, Bone the sofa; Locker took a sandwich, and Carey provided him with a small table for his cup and plate. Bone said to the proffered goodies, "I've had tea, thank you," and Locker looked lugubrious, eyeing the cake. "But Inspector Locker," Bone added, "must be starving." He avoided Locker's glance and drank tea.

"What do you want to know about?" Jem asked, tucking himself into the other corner of the sofa near the trolley.

"Tsk," said Carey.

"Why is it tsk? They're here on business, Carey. It's not a social occasion. *I'm* starving. School lunch was grissoles and canned carrots, and rhubarb crumble all burnt."

"Grissoles?" Bone enquired. The thin

face turned. The word had been bait and Jem was glad to have got a rise.

"Rissoles of gristle. Grissoles. And the rhubarb is raw lumps in sugar syrup, with burnt dry sand on top."

"Delicious," Bone said. "It's a great tradition, school meals. I should be sorry if they ever succeed in reforming it."

Jem grinned, with his head on one side, and took another sandwich.

Ken Cryer appeared on the terrace and tried the door. Jem, forcing half the sandwich into his mouth with the palm of one hand, flew to open it, first flipping a switch on the wall that presumably was an alarm. Cryer closed the switch when he had come in and shut the door. He loped to the trolley and took a cup from Carey.

Cryer was a heavily-used version of his son. His hands, at first sight grimy, were smeared with charcoal.

"Asking Jem about his unfortunate find?" He had a speaking voice mildly London without being Cockney. His singing voice Bone knew from Cha's records to be flexible and wide-ranging, the accent mid-Atlantic.

"We'd like to hear exactly why, when and how," Bone said.

"I'm sure Jem can manage that," said Carey, "though perhaps when he's had his tea."

"Mustn't talk with the mouth full," Jem said with a heavy shake of the head. "Uh *uh*."

She was about to speak when Cryer said, "Thank you very much, Carey. You won't want to hear this, I know. I'll look after the teapot."

She was flustered and got up bridling, and Bone watched Cryer turn on the charm as he took her to the door, crowded her to the door almost, and opened it for her. She went out smiling. Cryer drank from his cup on the way back, and sank into her chair, saying, "Right then, Jem. Get outside some cake and answer the questions. And you . . ." he swivelled round with the cake plate towards the others. "As usual, I'm forgetting the social bit. I met Inspector Locker last night, but—?"

"Detective-Superintendent Bone."

Predictably, Jem woke to the beauty of this surname. He breathed "Bone" and then caught his father's eye and took a sandwich doucely. "Why, when and how," Cryer prompted.

"Well *why*, because we thought it would be really triff to find her. I didn't think we would, what with people looking everywhere already. It was a sort of a game, I mean. Nanny wouldn't have come this far, we thought; I mean, lately she didn't ever walk this far, but she used to. She used to show me all sorts of things about insects and birds, and where there were places you could make dens, and things. She used to tell long stories on walks, too, I mean like serial stories, when I was younger."

He looked suddenly to see if that was laughable. Reassured, he went on: "When, it was Friday afternoon, that's games and I don't because of my leg so I was home, and Mona wasn't at school anyway, I think she had half-term, ours is next week. She came up here because she knew I'd be at home."

"She's younger than you, isn't she?"

"Yes, and she's a bit odd."

Cryer steered the sandwiches to Locker again. He had lit a cigarette, and now lay back in the armchair listening. Locker took notes, managing food, notebook and biro with his usual skill. Bone did not question the "bit odd", but nodded.

"She's not stupid," Jem pursued.

"I've met her," Bone agreed.

"Oh. Well, we saw wheel tracks and we pretended it was a villain. I sh'think it was police cars. We went along the little paths and then Prices started barking. That's my dog. Fat-Stock Prices."

"A terrier," Cryer supplied. He was pulling on the cigarette and watching his son.

"That's a good name," Bone said.

"He's rather rounded, you see. Particu'ly when he was a puppy. I think Sim, he's our cook, I think Sim feeds him too much. So he barked, and we saw he'd found something. It looked like old clothes. I thought if it *was* her, perhaps Mona oughtn't to see, but what can you do? She came anyway. It was Na—Miss Gray all right, though it was, I mean, completely gruesome. But we were interested. I didn't let her see where the wrist was sort of chewed. Something had pushed the sleeve up. Well then the leaves blew off her face and it was, well, mostly not there and we ran. I thought I'd be sick but I wasn't. So we went, and there was this man in the phone box, and when I asked if he'd mind because it was important he just was rude and shut the door."

"Should have had Jo with you."

"Yes well. Anyway we went straight to the police station. Nobody had really searched those woods because Nanny hadn't for ages walked this far but we didn't honestly think we'd find her."

"No. It wasn't likely, but you did. When Miss Gray was here, what was she like? Fierce, soft, whatever?"

"Oh, she was nice."

Cryer relaxed at the change of line. His sweater slid up as he settled further into the chair, and showed a lean brown midriff.

"She was strict, wasn't she, Dad?"

"Bedtime nine o'clock, not five past."

"You completely had to toe the line, I mean. But she was fair, she always was fair, she listened to your reasons."

"What did *you* feel about her as a nanny, Mr. Cryer?"

"I could leave her a free hand with Jem."

"And Dad's a fusspot about me." Jem gave his father a confident smile, happy in being the object of anxiety. Cryer pulled down his mouth corners.

"I admit it. I could leave Jem to her, though; and she was perfect when Jem did his leg at school. Greenstick but compound shin fracture. She wired me, went there, was with him in hospital, and being a nurse she was onto everything they did and couldn't be fobbed off as lay people can; what's more she got the nurses on her side. They let him come home sooner than they might have done, too, because the specialist could rely on her. We thought a lot of Nanny . . . She could keep shtum, too; people always ask about me, and not just reporters either. She never let on I wasn't on drugs. No word of my lack of group sex got past Nanny."

"She'd purse her lips and say 'Mr. Cryer's private life is absolutely his own affair,' and everyone thought the worst." Jem revelled in the thought.

Bone, hearing the tension in Cryer's voice in talking of Jem's leg, considered himself and Cha. The single parent. His sister was no Nanny Gray.

"But Nanny was fun," Jem said. "She used to tell stories when I couldn't sleep. Elephants and ogres and old ruins and werewolves. You'd think she'd think they'd be bad for me. She really understood. And nobody makes Welsh rabbit like she did. She *taught* Carey but somehow Carey doesn't do it right, they're always dry. Actually and not because of just that of course, I mind very much about Nanny. It's not going to be nearly so nice without her to go to. What was so awful, in the wood, the foxes and things doing that to her, when she'd been such a nice person. They didn't know, I mean. They couldn't help it. I can't say what I mean really."

Cryer splayed his arms akimbo on the chair arms and hoisted himself abruptly. The midriff vanished. Jem, glancing at his father, received a sleepy look through smoke. Bone thought, we would protect them from bad things; but they convert it all to their own knowledge.

"It's all right, Dad," Jem said to his father.

Bone was of a sudden irrationally hopeful of the human condition.

"Carey says too, it doesn't matter to people what happens to their bodies after they're dead. They leave their bodies."

"Which happens between three and twenty days, according to their religion."

"Yes," Bone said. "I've been aware of the same thing." He spoke almost absently, and had no glimmering that with the statement Ken Cryer had recognised him as a person. Up to that point, he had been a decent enough copper, skilful with children.

Bone saw that Cryer had started to watch him, but Cryer's eyes, narrowed because of cigarette smoke and incipient myopia, looked hostile. He supposed that his observation had been taken ill.

"Can you remember when it was that you last saw Miss Gray alive? When was it?"

Jem thought. His face began to show distress. "I think it was last Saturday. We —Jo and me—gave her a lift from the library down to Mouse Corner. It was lunch time so we didn't go into her house. And now we won't any more."

93

Bone stood up. Locker had finished a slice, ordinal number unknown, of chocolate cake, and got up too.

"Thank you, Jem. You've been very clear."

"I'll see you to the door," Cryer said. "No, finish your tea, Jemmy." On the way through the hall he said to Bone, "You're not a local inhabitant, are you?"

"No. Tunbridge Wells."

"We must go there more often," said Cryer obscurely, and opened the front door. Despite his command, Jem had followed.

Bone shook hands with Jem, and found Cryer's hand extended. Some Cryer charm was being employed as he asked, "Isn't a Superintendent rather a big fish?"

"Oh no. You're thinking of a Detective Chief Superintendent." He warmed to the charm in spite of himself. "He's the big fish."

Jem, still subdued by his memory of Nanny Gray alive, waved wanly and retired, as Locker climbed behind the wheel. Cryer stood at the door until they drove off.

"What was that 'We must visit

Tunbridge Wells more often' guff?"
Locker asked.

"Some private joke of his, I should
think. When did Cryer himself last see
Nanny?"

"He thought it was several weeks ago,
when she came to lunch. She called it
luncheon, he said. When I got here late
last night, he was most bothered about
whether the car would have woken Jem.
He was very wrought up about the boy
having discovered the body himself,
and of course it's a horrible thing. Miss
Sidgwick says he fusses over the boy."

Bone tried to put aside considerations
about single parents and keep his mind on
the case. He hoped Alison would have
insisted on Charlotte's going down the
road to her house for tea. The cousins
were boring, it was true . . .

"So far," he said resolutely, "the
obvious suspects are slightly outside
chances. Carey S could have, and is nicely
equipped with motive. She did see Nanny
Gray on the Tuesday, and wasn't too keen
on reporting her missing on Wednesday
until Playfair made her. Then there's the
Abdus, and the undisclosed reason for

what Playfair thinks is a hold Nanny had on the woman."

"Larkin?" Locker submitted doubtfully. "Nice enough bloke but form for GBH and is given to sudden violence."

"It's too soon to eliminate anyone."

"Or there's persons unknown."

"The world is full of them," said Bone.

Charlotte came from the sitting room to hug him. With his arms round her fragility he remembered Petra's sturdiness. Charlotte had inherited more from him than from her mother, but he hoped that some of Petra's vigour had been transmitted. He could smell the fusty warmth of Cha's hair and, from the kitchen, a scent of toast. At least Cha could eat now. He hung up his coat and followed her into the small kitchen, where her books were spread on the table.

"Did you have tea?"

"It's been a tea day," he said. "Steve got two and I'm awash with cuppas."

"It must be cupsa."

"Cupsa-daisy," he tried. She put on a face. She was wearing her hair in a small bun on top these days, emphasising the roundness of her forehead, the slightness of her neck. "Disgusted—" he said.

"—Of Tunbridge Wells. I'm doing us soup and sc-rambled eggs on toast, OK?" To his ear, she spoke all but normally when she wasn't under stress. Comments from his sister and from the school surprised him, and he could only suppose she was under least strain when alone with him; a gratifying conclusion.

The soup steamed. He carried the tray and set its contents out on the living room table. Cha brought the soup. They settled amicably. The flat, he realised, had at last begun to feel like home, not like a make-do, for their amputated family.

The telephone jangled. He said, "Oh damn" and reached out, gave the number grudgingly. The caller's voice, however, recognised no obstacles.

"Val Herne here. That's Chief Inspector Bone?"

"Detective Superintendent . . ."

"Yes yes. Sorry to bother you at home," the voice pursued insincerely. It was a voice that expected its requirements to be no bother. "I'm concerned about this enquiry into Nanny—into Mrs. Gray's death, so I got hold of your home number. Am I to understand there's some *question* about her death?"

"Always an enquiry into sudden death, Sir Valentine."

Charlotte covered her mouth in ostentatious suppression of mirth. The voice imperiously went on in his ear. "I quite fail to understand. Nobody could think of foul play. The Sidgwick girl said that Nanny hit her head and then wandered off into the woods. There surely can't be any suggestion of foul play?"

"It's routine, Sir Valentine."

Cha inverted a small plate over his soup bowl. He smiled at her.

"I'd have enquired before, but I'm still infernally occupied with my brother's affairs. I rang Carey to find what was going on and she tells me the place is swarming with police . . ."

Infernally occupied? Bone hoped that the late Sir Gareth was not in a like position.

". . . He left everything in a tangle, an incredible mess. He really couldn't cope with life."

The chap doth protest too much. Does

he feel he hasn't shown enough concern for Miss Gray? He'd called her "Mrs.", too.

"I haven't—hadn't seen Nanny for ages. I hardly liked, y'know, to face her after Gareth died. She'd so much rather it had been me that I felt distinctly *de trop*. Also I felt it might be painful to her as we're superficially so much alike."

Bone had uncovered and gone on with his soup, since the baronet showed a readiness to keep talking. Admittedly he felt also a touch of defiance at the assumption that his time was at Sir Valentine's disposal. Charlotte mimed "do you want more?" and he shook his head. She went out.

"Are you there?" demanded the voice.

"Certainly."

"What have these 'investigations' turned up so far?"

"It's still a matter for official enquiry, Sir Valentine."

The ego at the far end caught the hint, didn't like it. "The matter's very much my concern. Nanny Gray was a member of the family. That little house of hers belonged to us."

"I'd like to discuss the matter."

"I've told you how busy I am with my brother's affairs. And that I have not seen her for quite some time. What else do you need to know? I'm quite ready."

"It's never very satisfactory to conduct these things over the telephone, Sir Valentine."

"You don't want me to come to the station, do you?" The voice sounded almost intrigued by the idea.

"No, sir. I could come to see you."

"Oh, I suppose it could be managed. I'm going through my diary . . ."

"Tomorrow, sir?"

"To—oh. M'm. Well. I suppose I can put off . . . look, come over for a drink at twelve tomorrow, Bone."

"Very well, sir. Thank you. Tomorrow at twelve. I'll be bringing Inspector Locker."

The voice made an OK-yah reply and rang off.

"Is he truly Sir Valentine, Daddy?"

"Truly."

"Sir Valentine! He might as well be called Sir Michaelmas or Sir Boxing Day."

She was buttering toast in the kitchen. "You didn't like him."

"I don't know him. On that acquaintance, though, not charming."

"Sir Christmas," she said.

"Ah, but there was one. Christmas Humphries. Famous lawyer and judge."

"Stone the crows. Did you meet nice people today?"

"Ken Cryer."

She appeared in the doorway. "No, did you? Did you? Oh, don't tell me. Don't tell me any bit about him. He will be ordinary; he ought to be all silver lamé and surrounded by adoring girls."

"I won't tell you a thing. He did strike me as being a nice sort."

"Not glam."

"No silver lamé but I wouldn't say no glamour. It's probably quite spurious but it's there. He could step out in silver lamé and not look silly. His songs have often struck me as intelligent, too."

"Did you tell him?"

"It wasn't that kind of conversation."

"Sort of 'When did you last see your Nanny'?"

"Quite."

She brought in the scrambled egg on toast, with its mushrooms and tomatoes. "You ought to tell him a-bout his songs. Bet he'd like it."

"You're prejudiced, pet. Ken Cryer isn't going to care if a country cop likes his lyrics."

Her dark-blue eyes lit up. "Alliteration."

"Yes. Fortuitous."

"Later on, will you hear my lines?"

"Of course."

She soon went back to her prep at the other table. He peeled an orange, laid the pigs in a circle round a saucer and took it through. This was because she was working. Undoing an orange was an exercise in coordination and apt to be messy, but it was an exercise and useful; he had to leave her, usually, to do it. She looked up with that singularly radiant smile of hers; her own invention, Petra had none such.

"Ta."

She opened one of her exercise books, found the place, and held it up for him to see, pointing at the red ink comment.

Good. I like your ideas.

Yes, he thought, regarding her bent head. How much I agree.

He called Locker with the date for tomorrow. Steve was philosophical because it was his duty Sunday anyway, so he lost no time by being on a case. Bone was not so lucky.

He also made a call to Sam Pearsall. "I need to pick your brains a bit, please."

"Legal tangles for you? Personal or official?"

"Official."

"I have to be in tomorrow morning. Want to come to the office?"

"Ideal," Bone said.

6

ON Sunday morning he dressed with some hesitation. "What do you suppose one wears for a Sunday morning visit to a baronet?"

Cha killed the vacuum cleaner's moan and came to look at the wardrobe. "Not a lot of choosing."

"No. Not best suit. Blowed if I will."

"Brown one."

"Hope it won't be cold. It's clean, not new, not smart."

She picked out the brown worsted tie with small cream dots she had given him last year. Charlotte was good at ties, scarves and socks, he never had to take her choices back for exchange. Petra used to buy her own taste, not his: ties like Neapolitan ice-cream, light blue socks. Wives cherish hopes of remodelling their men.

"Pity I haven't got some thundering good old school tie like a fictional detective."

"You're good-looking enough to be a pop star, why worry?"

"A bit old for one, surely?"

"What about Jagger? You're better-looking 'n Ken Cryer."

"Fibber. Now, I should have a lamé jacket. That would be in such crashing bad taste it would make no end of an impression."

She giggled, holding his coat as he tied the tie, surveying him in the glass. She tilted her head and became serious. This morning she had fastened her hair back on her crown with a huge black butterfly grip.

"What's on, today, with you?" he asked.

"Do the living room. Lunch with Aunt Alison. Grue comes in the afternoon, play some records."

"Good. Take care."

She stood on the doorstep and waved as he walked off. Petra used to stand there, sometimes lifting her face to the day. Petra used to taste weather. It had been raining that day, when the side of the car had been sheared away where she and the baby had been.

He had called at the archives to look at

Gareth Herne: overdose ... 30th September ... found by Palmerston, butler, in family coach in old coach house ... This final circumstance appealed to Bone.

He came out onto the street into welcome sunlight. A little mean wind searched his neck and ears and ankles, and convinced him that the brown suit was too thin. He looked at the few sturdy clouds high overhead. The shopping precinct had a Sunday emptiness still. He crossed at the Army and Navy to go down Mount Pleasant Road.

The space of it was pleasant. Here you could look into distance past the plunge of the hill. The Town Hall had been constructed during a period of architectural dignity, at least, back from the road to let itself be seen, and to allow a display of civic flowers, in season. Bone turned right, into a street of Georgian houses. When they were built, the proportion of the street must have been good as well; now, a car dormitory, it offered cramped pavements and poor access. He had reached Sam Pearsall's doorway and was finding, from his watch, that he was as usual early, when a Wolsey double-parked, blocking the street. The driver swung out, edged between parked cars and loomed towards him, a key held poised for the lock. Sam Pearsall said, "I'll let you in and find a slot for the chariot." There was not room for him and Bone on the doorstep so Bone stood on the pavement until the door was open and Sam had turned round. He pressed the keys into Bone's hand. "Go on up. Make yourself at home. Be five minutes with luck."

A Renault stopped, panting. Pearsall raised a benign paw and lumbered back to clear the road.

Bone pushed the door to, climbed the beige carpet past uniform framed seascapes that must have been bought by the dozen; the building held a quiet, discreet air, professionally reticent, not breathing anything in confidence. On the first floor, Pearsall's door was in a partition that spoiled the landing's proper space. A second key let Bone into a cubbyhole with coat hooks, and a further sorting of the jailer's dozen on Pearsall's key ring let him into the office. Bone put the keys on the desk before he could pocket and walk off with them. The room was close, all but anonymous: a desk, two grey filing cabinets, an easy chair and a hard chair; on the desk a pen set, two telephones, blotter, and a vase of elderly yellow and bronze chrysanthemums showing a withered edge to their ruffs. Behind the desk rose a curved and padded luxurious executive chair. It and the pictures were more like Pearsall's choice. Bone walked round looking at them again, for on previous visits he had not had leisure or opportunity to enjoy them. There were Victorian and Edwardian photographs of Kent—hop-pickers, Cranbrook windmill and Stone Street, the Pantiles, Folkestone Bandstand on the Leas; the Marine Parade at Dover in 1894, Margate Beach in 1860, Mercery Lane in Canterbury, the only unchanged place; and a map of Tudor Kent.

Pearsall climbed the stairs and invaded the room. He dressed in an almost clerical grey, his waistcoat in basalt folds across its generous swell.

"Coffee," he said, and as it was a cry from the heart rather than an invitation, Bone did not demur.

"Sit down, Robert. Don't stand about

like impending doom. Suppose by profession you're impending doom for someone, but not here. Now—" he plunged into the next room and could be heard tinkering about. "Where does the woman put the thing? Too much damned tidiness. If she'd leave things out I could—" He came back with the kettle and its cord, plugged it in by the filing cabinet on which he perched it, and grumbled his way out again. Bone identified the sounds, clashing china, a fridge door, a drawer, and Pearsall emerged with two mugs in one hand, a coffee jar under one arm, and a milk bottle. "Don't mind mugs, I hope? We have a delicate china set for delicate ladies. I need more than that. Got plenty of time?"

"Enough."

"Good man." Pearsall swung his head at the kettle, which started to hum.

Having made coffee, Sam lowered himself into the vast chair, swivelled round, and then back to lever himself out and get files from the cabinet, sat down again, changed his spectacles for a half-moon pair and squared off the files before him. He drank what must have been a scalding mouthful from his mug. Bone, who had started to warm his hands on his own mug, had given up on finding the earthenware far too hot. Pearsall sat back, saying, "Now then." He looked like Samuel Whiskers and might benignly be watching Tom Kitten trussed up.

"Miss Gray's estate," he went on. "An interesting subject. The Will's not proven, of course. Can't therefore tell you anything worth knowing, though I *was* going to see her this week. Wednesday. She telephoned on the twenty-seventh. She didn't say what it was but it would be about property . . . Sir Gareth Herne's estate, that is another matter. He'd previously given the house, Mouse Cottage, to Miss Gray and that's well out of duties, but here," he was leafing through pages and put a finger down, "a massive bequest for a woman in her circumstances. It wasn't a surprise to her when I communicated the facts to her on his death, as he had informed her already. The bequest was no surprise, that is. The amount of it was."

"M'm?"

"Two hundred thousand pounds."

After a moment, Bone said, "And she never had the benefit of it."

"She said to me, 'Well, I can spend a little on being more comfortable,' and I hope she did. She'd been a hard-working woman and earned a comfortable life."

Bone's coffee was now cool enough to drink. Sam took his own mug to the kettle for more. "For you? No?" His head swung towards Bone. "A motive, undoubtedly, so much money, though who thought they could get any of it was another matter, eh? And Herne was of sound mind when he made his Will. Knew him reasonably well. I've seen him drugged. He wasn't, when I went there to take his directions." Back at the desk, sidling behind it and taking the chair, he looked over his spectacles again, Churchillian, and went on, "He didn't pick his words. He told me there'd been another quarrel with his brother, but that he'd waited until he was cooler before he'd got in touch with me. A clever man in such things, Gareth. He was abusive of his brother but not heated. Had to leave the Hall to Valentine. Entailed. He grudged that. 'Might as well bring in gorillas and set them to playing the drawing room piano. Says he loves the place but he wants it as a showpiece, money-grubbing little pissarse.' Which is, Robert, not of forensic use but indicates the terms they were on. My reason for the quotation. And then Valentine's wife, 'Lady Muck' though, bound to remark, he altered the initial M for a deleterious substitute further on in the conversation. 'Val and Lady Muck want to go the full commercial, to offer bed, breakfast, butler and buggerall, the Great Fourposter Racket.'"

Bone heard the inverted commas pincering the phrases as they emerged from the solicitor's mouth.

"This was, I may say, Sir Gareth's opinion. I have no personal knowledge of either such a plan, or of the character of the present Lady Herne. Not often met her."

Appreciating this professional exactitude, Bone said, "Yes, I understand. So Miss Gray was to enjoy this considerable sum."

"And that alters things?"

"M'm." Bone drank coffee.

"We have our professional reticences. More coffee?"

"No, thank you. Do you know how Sir Valentine took the news of this bequest?"

"I communicated it to him by letter. I received no reply."

"Did Sir Gareth give his reasons for leaving a 'massive sum' to Miss Gray?"

"His words were, so far as I can recall them after six months, 'She cared for me. She brought me up to the best of her ability and it's not her fault she failed. I am my own failure. She was the only one who cared for me.'"

"That's bitter," said Bone, afflicted.

"The worse for being, to the best of my belief, true." Sam Pearsall gave a brisk to-and-fro to his nose end with a flat forefinger. "He said once, 'I pay for my pleasures, God knows, but never a penny more than they're worth.' Yes. I fear he had a sour mouth and a sick look for that."

Bone thought: Sir Gareth Herne must have had great charm. This man was fond of him.

"Were the brothers physically alike?"

"Superficially. Gareth a little taller. Similar colouring and build. Not at all alike in manner though both can—could

113

—be very pleasant to get on with. Gareth's death, a somewhat *outré* location. You know the story?"

"He got hold of some uncut heroin, I understand."

"I would have thought that wasn't very easy."

"It's less difficult than we'd like."

"And in that old coach house. Reminds me of *A Tale of Two Cities*, you know?"

"The Marquis was in his bed, though," Bone said, "but I remember the notice pinned to him with the knife."

"'Drive him fast to his grave'—Gareth did his own driving." Pearsall finished his coffee. "I understand Sir Valentine intends to set up a carriage museum for tourists."

There flashed upon Bone's inward eye the preposterous vision of a throng of tourists peering into the dark recesses of a coach, where a Madame Tussaud's figure lolled, glass eyes shining.

In the silence, while Pearsall brooded over the untouched files, Bone brought his mind back to the case. "So that Miss Gray's niece possibly stands to inherit quite something?"

"Possibly. I make no statement, for

Miss Gray's Will has yet to be proved. A pleasant girl, the niece, not as intelligent as the aunt, but of course inexperienced. One can mistake that for lack of intelligence." His tone was not convinced.

"I should rather think," Bone said absently, "that it's intelligence which makes use of experience." Unless Carey Sidgwick needed a large sum of money in a hurry, she had no motive. It looked as though she had only to wait, or even perhaps only to ask for a loan from her affectionate aunt. She might have asked, and been refused. Enquire, went his mental note, whether she has any scheme in hand demanding instant capital.

"Is the niece your client?"

"Sidgwick? No. Miss Gray brought her one day and kindly remarked to her that when she needed someone to look after her affairs for her she could do worse than come to me."

"Were those her words?" Bone asked, smiling.

"I believe she said the girl 'couldn't do better . . .'"

"A small, vital, difference. Well, thank you Sam." He stood up. "It was very good of you to give me this time today; your weekend should be your own."

"Yours isn't," Sam said. "Glad to come in, on just the basis that my weekend should be my own. We have the grandchildren, if you please, and I've a client coming up before the JP on Monday, need to put in some work on his case."

"I'll let myself out." Bone saw that Pearsall was preparing to rise.

"I will not deny that it would be a kindness on your part. I'm no friend to those stairs."

The wind in the street was downright boisterous. Bone set off to fetch the car and pick up Locker. They would be in nice time at Herne Hall.

Locker was in a Sunday suit.

The Herne Hall drive started where a big field gate stood open over a cattle grid between tall white wooden posts. A wicket gate at the side would let foot passengers through onto a path past the grid, but as the road, or drive, seemed to lead interminably out of sight there weren't likely to be many walkers. The old lodge was a half mile back along the road, with its graceful brick bay, but where iron gates must have stood had been walled up, with a little postern for lodge tenants. This drive was, presumably, more direct.

Parkland on both sides rolled authentically, here and there punctuated with trees —cedar, a row of poplars—more sparsely than the eye required. Had they been selling off timber? The smart asphalt road ran straight across, switchbacking a little over rises, and joined an older, wider carriage road that topped a rise and gave, on the opposite rise of a little valley supplied with a natural-looking stretch of water, a view of the house: Georgian, blessing the eye with its proportions, its thorough suitability to the site chosen. Stable wing one side, with a small bell-house on the outer end of the roof. Orangery, was it, on the balancing side, with a cupola? It was not a large place, unless you were trying to run it in modern times. It was a gentleman's residence, as in Bone's books on architecture, built in a day when a gentleman might make a fortune and spend it, naturally, on land, and during one of the few periods in human history when what was fashionable to build was also simple and full of harmony; natural bad taste, in that era, had not had a lot of chance.

As Locker circled the drive over crackling gravel, Bone took in the peeling paint on the façade's woodwork, weeds in the flowerbeds beneath, grass borders fraying into the paths.

Locker, whose face had betrayed no impression throughout, ducked to straighten his tie in the wing mirror as he got out. He said without moving his lips, "Eh, guv, you sure we got the right entrance?"

Bone pulled an iron stirrup handle beside the door. For a long few minutes they stood there, a chill wind playing round their legs. The car ticked. "Ring again?" Locker suggested.

The door opened. The butler, looking over their shoulders for the cat whose job it was to bring them in, resembled Gielgud doing a cameo part; an inexpertly carved cameo, perhaps. Bone gave their names and he allowed them in, shut the door with soundless care and waited. Bone at once started taking his coat off; this was a social visit, the butler had intimated, and he relieved Bone of the overcoat, took Locker's as he hurriedly shed it, disposed of them over a carved chest and moved forward saying to the air, "Sir Valentine is in the conservatory. This way, if you please."

"Or if you don't," Locker murmured. Bone hoped it had not shown that he was ignorant about coats, was too used to Police Enquiries where one wasn't a guest. Then it struck him that etiquette was constructed to put you down, to separate Us from Them. He relaxed. It was an obstacle course they didn't want you to surmount.

From the hall (black and white marble, with an undistinguished, journeyman full-length of an eighteenth century Herne over the chimneypiece), they re-entered human life, a sitting room with red silk wall coverings. The chairs' brocade might be thin and fraying, a gesso table scorched and ring-marked, but this room was used, inhabited, gave comfort.

Beyond the french windows, in the pale light of a glass roof, a man was fiddling with a drinks trolley among the ferns and palms. The butler opened the french windows, said, "Mr. Bone, Mr. Locker, sir," and withdrew. Sir Valentine, fielding a toppling bottle, swore and then turned. Smooth as Ken Cryer's, the charm came on like a searchlight.

He was far younger than his voice had sounded. Was it Sir Dorian, with his picture in the attic, by Zoffany retouched by Francis Bacon? Letting the idea lie in his mind, Bone went through the greetings. Sir Valentine indicated a chair, letting Locker find himself one. His face still gave Bone that sense of not being what it seemed. He wore a scarf, as if to hide the neck that betrays age faster than faces do. Perhaps this curious look had always been his, of course, had been the reason Nanny thought misdeeds and escapades his fault.

He handed Bone the orange and soda he asked for, with a minimal incredulity over his refusing alcohol. Locker he accorded the treatment a bad shop assistant gives, lifting his chin at him with the implied "Wotcher want then?" So much for the innate courtesy of the upper classes, Bone mused as he watched the pallid orange soda, more Sch than orange, passed to Locker.

"Glad you found your way. I realised I hadn't explained about the new entrance. I suppose you people are always up-to-date on these things."

Bone made a reply without comment on the apparent confusion over the different branches of police work, and allotting full marks to Locker for having in fact known.

"Well. How are things going?"

"We are establishing facts, Sir Valentine. When would it be that you last saw Miss Gray personally?"

"Can one see one's old Nanny impersonally? Miss—we called her 'Mrs.' Gray, you know. A convention; old servants."

Bone had thought this was reserved for housekeepers, but didn't say so. He began to feel defensively plebeian.

"Well then. Of course I went to see her as a duty from time to time. I've always been fond of the old thing, but it was Gareth who adored her. Always running to have his face wiped and be told he was a good boy really. Not that he *was*." Sir Valentine's eyebrows shot up in mock dismay, he sighed, shrugged and glanced at Locker in a pas-devant way. "It must be common property now, though. It was all pretty painful."

The empty, neatly good-looking face became plaintive. Bone thought: it plainly hurt Sir Gareth more than it hurt you.

"My brother was not a good boy at all. I must say he had some appalling friends. And a habit. He'd become quite unreliable. You will be used to this sort of story but to families like ours it's a shock. A horrible shock."

It's a shock in any family, Bone thought; but of course the rich are more sensitive, aren't they? Once only the rich could afford to mess up their lives spectacularly. What are we coming to when it's the Cryers of this world who can be expected to be on drugs and to OD for an exit.

"So as I told you on the telephone, we're trying to clear up the muddle he left. Papers in disorder, bills and receipts . . ."

At least there were receipts. Bone had helped a colleague's widow to sort her late husband's affairs and there had not been a receipt in the house.

"I don't know how we're to keep this."

His eyes rolled like the parkland and he gestured. Beyond his shoulder, Locker too rolled his eyes and half-flicked a gesture. He knew Bone's command of feature.

"So when did you last see Mrs. Gray?"

"My good man, I was telling you. I don't know. It must be weeks. Of course I do go, did go, from time to time. I have to go through Saxhurst every so often, but one can't always stop. Nanny's little car was usually in the only parking place nearby. And then, well, though I loved her dearly I wasn't the most welcome person in her life and besides, the old thing could be very tedious. They don't realise one has grown up."

And has one? Bone wondered. The glass doors swung and Lady Herne arrived, profusely.

"So *sorry* not be here. I was on the phone to the most difficult—"

Locker, rising, sent a plant pot to the tiles, unhousing a tired fern and a pound or two of loam. He apologised and set about putting it back, but he had spoiled her entrance. Her acid regard of him changed instantly to roguishness when she caught Bone's eye. "Trying to make an appointment with my dentist, but he's like *Cats*, you know, one has to book years ahead. He spends weeks in the Middle East doing the whole household of this sheikh and that. An old friend! Doesn't mind my getting at him on Sundays."

She sat down in her husband's chair and looked Bone over. The men sat again, Bone realising that she was, rather obviously, finding him tasty. She gave him an oddly collusive little smile. Her husband nudged her shoulder with a glass and she took it without a glance and sat there exuding scent and sex inappropriately. She was long-limbed and elegant, dressed in designer dustbin, a jumpsuit of faded tan, boots well-worn but expensive, a sweater that might be Missoni in earth colours, and an appearance of not being made up that probably took hours.

The drink her husband had provided was a zonk of gin, with a tinge of pink as if a mosquito had bled in it. She sank some and said, "What a delicious name you have. Though you must have gone through hell at school. Bo-one! It inspires absolute confidence."

"How fortunate," he said with protective stolidity. Lady Herne playing social games was not about to get him as opponent, partner, team-mate or, conceivably, quarry. He tried to dismiss Pearsall's report of her brother-in-law's sobriquet for her from his mind.

"Did you know Miss—Mrs. Gray, Lady Herne?"

"Oh, not well. One had the feeling that she didn't approve. At least I wasn't attempting to be Gareth's wife, for which only a Royal would have been suitable, with the temperament of one of the more nauseating saints, for sure." Lady Herne put a hand to her heart and turned her eyes upwards in a brief neat caricature of a religious picture. She drank. "Perhaps that's a little near speaking ill of the dead. Valentine wanted Nanny to live here. In her own flat, you know, completely independent, but massively more comfortable and much safer. I mean if she'd fallen over here, with that twitchy disease of hers, someone would have spotted her right away, doctors and so on, no wandering off into the woods, poor thing."

"I kept urging her," said Sir Valentine. "I wasn't her Gareth, but we could have looked after her here. There's masses of room, no one would have got in anyone's hair."

"Val worried so. He goes on about how awkward she could be, but he was really concerned. That weekend before she died he'd been ringing and ringing her."

Sir Valentine had brought forward a rather horrid white iron chair with pink squab cushions. He sprang up now to fuss over people's glasses and had another try at getting Bone or Locker to have "a proper drink". A large pale dog, hitherto disguised as an old roll of carpet, raised its head, then lumbered to its feet. A waft of dog-smelling warm air reached Bone. It had been lying on a grating, and the odd choice of venue for the reception was explained. This place, of necessity heated, was perhaps the warmest room in the house.

"I did worry," said Sir Valentine. "Though she was indomitable she was getting frail. Very frail. I worried. I was, in spite of everything, attached to her." He spoke as if it were challenged, as if such magnanimity were hardly to be expected.

"What did she say?"

"Say? When?"

"On the telephone."

"Oh, she didn't answer. There was no answer."

"Was that usual?"

"Oh, fairly. She could be very bolshie, darling Nanny."

"She did answer, though, darling. I remember because you were terribly upset and wouldn't tell me what she said."

"No no," as if she were a child who had spoken out of turn. "It was a wrong number. It was upsetting. Some village idiot. I did not at first hear that it was a child who said 'Hullo'. I said 'Nanny?' and this infernal child said 'Nanny's dead' and rang off. I was very upset of course. I rang Carey at the Manor. She said," and he sounded almost outraged by it, "that Nanny was perfectly all right, just resting after one of her falls."

"You were like a cat on hot bricks all day after that."

"I was wondering if I should go over. And you know perfectly well I had other things to worry about." His tone warned her, but she laughed and went on.

"The estimate for the roof! It arrived that day. This place, you must know, Mr. Bone," and again her voice made a tease of the name, "is ker-*rumbling*. Actually, we called at Nanny's on the way to Ken's party. There wasn't any answer and the house was dark, but Val went round to the back and there was a light in the bedroom; so he called to her that it was him; but she must have been asleep, so we came away. At Kenny's, Carey said Nanny was in bed, she'd been shaky but the rather weird Playfair woman was going to call in, she had the key, and not to worry. So Val was relieved and we had a nice party. In fact Val really had a *party*, I had to drive back."

"It wasn't till Thursday that anyone thought to tell us she was missing."

"Wednesday evening, darling." She held out her glass to her husband without looking. He took it. "Wednesday evening the girl telephoned to know if Nanny was here. As if she could be!"

He replaced the filled glass in her hand, had yet another go at getting alcohol into Bone and Locker, snorted incredulously once more, and sat down, with a slight error because the dog had been sitting against the chair and its weight had shifted it when Sir Valentine got up.

Bone had been trying to neutralise himself in the hope that more would be said, because a scenario was beginning to take shape, starting with a child's voice saying "Nanny's dead." On Monday, said Mona Staveley, she was dead, her hand was like wood. However, the Hernes seemed to have come to the end of the subject. He said "It's certainly odd about the child."

"Odd! Disgusting. An intolerable thing to say."

"Some children these days," Locker put in, "call their grandmother 'nanny' or 'nana'. This child might have thought you were asking for her grandmother."

They regarded him rather as if the plants had spoken, with slight puzzlement at his having a voice and intelligent thought.

"Oh. Yes. So they do. Absurd. But you can imagine . . ." Sir Valentine, faced with Locker's inexpressive expression, thought the words not appropriate and turned to Bone, "you can imagine how I felt when I heard it. And later, it seemed a dreadful coincidence."

Bone wanted more words about the property, wherein seemed Sir Valentine's real interest. The child's voice could wait. He looked around, at the plants and the view of the park. "It must be very hard these days to maintain a place to this standard. Do you have trouble getting staff?"

"Staff!" He almost yapped. "I could get them, if I could afford them. They're quite happy on the dole, and they want the earth if they've actually got to *work* for money."

"It seems odd of Sir Gareth to leave substantial sums of money away from the house." Bone thought that the substitution of 'house' for 'you' was masterly tact, and indeed it worked.

"Unbelievable, frankly. Typical of Gareth. Sentiment and impulse. Responsibility to the house where he grew up, which he'd owned, would seem the least one could expect but no! We have to pay death duties on it just the same, even though it all went to the woman who pampered that demanding ego of his."

"Val is *the* world's bore on his Freudian childhood. He and Gareth were for ever rocking the boat in the hope the other would fall overboard and drown."

"Rubbish. We argued, of course, and fought. Brothers always do. Gar was over-sensitive, took everything seriously, and she encouraged him. She did it all out of love, certainly, but the best intentions of mice and men as the saying has it . . . well, it was to my advantage. I had to grow up a lot faster than he did. I've had to be realistic. Since Gareth failed us we've had to buckle-to and make what we can of it. He wouldn't listen to anything while the house was his, but we are keen to make the place self-supporting and we don't lack for ideas. Yes, I admit," and his eyes were luminously blue as he envisioned it, "I hoped Nanny might be willing to help. I was unreasonable in that. She could have no real feeling for my situation. So we are where we are." He added, as Lady Herne pushed the dog's exploring head from her lap, "Fiona's a marvellous manager."

This crumb of approval elicited a surprised glance and then a quick mirthless smile from her. She rose, laid her hand on Bone's arm and said, "Come and see the nucleus of our little museum."

As he rose, she looked at his mouth, not his eyes. Sir Valentine surged to his feet, tripped on the dog, swore crudely and swung a foot into its gut so that it scampered limping and whimpering away.

Lady Herne ignored this display and Bone concluded it was not unusual. Perhaps the butler wore shinpads; he walked stiffly enough. Perhaps it was a marvel that Gareth and Valentine, quarrelling for so many years, had avoided crippling each other.

As they followed Lady Herne, she remarked to Locker over her shoulder, "There are several *very* delicate plants on this table." Locker, gently impassive, said, "Yes, m'lady."

Below-stairs passages in big houses, even when tarted up with white paint, new matting and prints of *Mariage à la Mode* and *Mr. Sponge's Sporting Tour*, always convey that they were intended for hurrying servants laden with trays, buckets, hot-water jugs, coals, slop pails and dirty linen. The windows are placed to give light, not to demonstrate a view, and have never been curtained. One door recess had been widened to allow one solid, oak, polished chair, in consideration for the abigail or footman who waited a life away hour after hour for the bell within. Further on, a door led through a lobby at the foot of stone back stairs to a coach house.

It was roomy and arched, not high. Two of the three great double doors had been boarded in and windowed, though the spaces as yet were filled with plastic sheeting. The cold was remarkable after the conservatory's heating, and the stone flags struck like ice through Bone's shoes.

A neat little early Austin, with its pram-hood roof and opening windscreen, stood shining upright at one side. Beyond it was a motorcycle, spindly in the old style, on its stand. A wicker Bath chair, relic perhaps of some gouty Herne, and a wicker pram on high thin wheels stood by the wall, under loops of harness and a painted wheel. A railed governess cart, with its gate and metal step behind, had American-cloth seats patched with plastic strips that nearly matched. To the left loomed the bulk of the family coach, given an odd, blank appearance because its blinds were drawn (in mourning?) behind the glass.

It was an impressive object, solid on fair-sized wheels, the curved springs graceful, the box rails shining. Its smart, dark-blue paint, with a heron crest on the door, was crackled.

The whitewashed walls of the coach house bore, besides harness, coaching prints that lacked relevance here. This had been a workplace for men who cleaned mud from paint and polished and leathered it; for upholsterers perhaps, and then a mechanic seeing to the maintenance of a Daimler.

Bone remained aware, as Sir Valentine rehearsed a dissertation on the place's glories, of two other claims on his attention: Lady Herne, coolly staring at him, and the great coach whose presence was, by association, macabre.

Sir Valentine went on to speak of vehicles he hoped to acquire, and Bone, playing stupid to Lady Herne's appraising eyes, grasped the handle of the coach and idly turned it. The door opened and with a series of sharp clacks the steps unfolded, hitting Bone's shin. Sir Valentine stopped in midspiel. He said "Ha-ha!" with real amusement.

"Don't you find it painful displaying this coach?" Bone asked blandly.

There was a lilting silence. Bone waited, enquiring, thick-skinned, while Sir Valentine, drawing his head back, seemed to convey that a gaffe had been made.

"In fact darling Gareth hardly left us any option," said Lady Herne after a moment, and she was amused. "Of course it'd be, what?—decorous to respect his memory, but here we are penniless and trying to make the most of what we've got. Which is this mausoleum piece."

Though he liked her choice of words, Bone had other intentions than to show any appreciation of her. He said, "I hope you didn't find him yourself, Sir Valentine," knowing he hadn't.

"God, no, Palmerston did. Of course he fetched me. Damn it, the whole thing must be in the police reports."

"Yes, sir. Of course. I'm sorry. It wasn't my case, you see. It must have been a severe shock to you."

"It was dreadful. Dreadful."

Bone folded up the little steps, tucked

them in their slot and shut the door. A sardonic wraith of his imagining regarded him from the far corner, needle in arm. He reflected that he had no idea where Sir Gareth had been sitting or lying. He had not examined the site sketch or photographs in the file.

"What else do you plan to have here, Sir Valentine?"

"I was telling you."

"Yes, sir, the early Morris and the curricle. Aren't curricles rather tall?"

"Plenty of room. Yes, yes."

"And a Rolls Silver Ghost," said Lady Herne under her breath."

"Do you use this motorbike at all?" Locker asked. Sir Valentine turned swiftly.

"No, no. Never. It works. Everything's in running order. There won't be any petrol. I've never used it."

"Should think one could still use it for buzzing about the neighbourhood. It looks in great condition, sir. But I see you couldn't, as it's got no indicators. It couldn't be licensed."

"Solely a museum exhibit."

"Do you ride a motorbike, Lady

Herne?" Locker asked. There was a silence.

As they got into their car, Bone said to Locker, "That was your second plant pot." They settled their seat belts and Bone started the engine. "What was in your mind about that motorbike?"

"Gravel in the tires. Mud and dust not quite cleaned off, like someone had gone over it with a cloth just. Not much of a museum, that place."

"Not yet; they need capital for sure. They could always exhume Sir Gareth and prop him there well pickled; it'd drum up a roaring trade."

Locker, after a moment's shocked protest, spluttered, "Well, it might. It'd be an improvement on pushchairs."

"Steve, that phone call and the child's pretty message . . ."

"Mona?"

"She said she saw Nanny in bed, dead."

"With a hand like wood. Suppose that was rigor, that's putting the death Sunday, Sunday night. Or does a catalepsy give rigor too?"

"Ask Foster. But the old lady wasn't dead in bed, was she?"

"Not according to Sidgwick. That girl's got some answers to give, if Mona was telling the truth."

They went slowly over the cattle grid and eased into the road.

"Do you think this case is going to get interesting, sir?"

It had interested Bone all along.

Bone sat over PC Berryman's typescript, which was commendably clear. The bright modernity of the Citizens' Advice Bureau had not borne the depredations of time well. Damp stains on the walls and ceiling, and a sag in the latter, were evidence to the effects of weather more violent than the architect had allowed for. Those stains, the stacking chairs with their crumbled corners and chipped paint, and the tiles with all their surface worn off, showed where funds had not been available. In the sixties people had planned for a world of expenditure. Bone, an inheritor of global blight, furled his coat round him and picked out information:

Two boys going from the local bus to the chippie on Monday evening had seen Miss Gray posting letters. They had seen her before at that time on Mondays and had seen her perfectly well by the street-lamp near the postbox. She had gone off towards her cottage "sharpish".

A Mrs. Stance had seen her "near the phone box", had hailed her and received a nod in response. She was not surprised, as Miss Gray did not always want to stop and talk. She was quite a fast walker though not as steady as she used to be. Very nifty on her pins and been a great walker in her day.

Harold Moss, grocer, said Miss Gray was bossy, gave advice gratuitously, telling him to reorganise his shelving as one of the centre stands made an obstacle course. Naturally he couldn't move his whole display, he was there to sell. Of course Miss Gray had to prove her point by falling onto the display the very next week and bursting cereal packets—cornflakes were still turning up in corners. He didn't know when he had last seen her. The place was full of old dears most days and a lot of them didn't like the self-service, they preferred to be helped, which he did when he could, but Miss Gray could manage on her own so he didn't notice her as a rule.

Post Office: Miss Gray always prompt to collect her pension until she came into that money. The last three weeks she hadn't taken it, and when she came in for stamps and they asked her, she said she did not think it right to accept state aid when she did not need it. She'd told Mrs. Higgins where she should put the sweets so that Mona Staveley couldn't reach them unseen. As if Mona was the only little light-fingers around! She told Higgins to give up smoking because of his cough. The Post Office smelt, she said, and everyone would be better off if he did. Then when Jason Higgins, seven, had measles and the doctor wouldn't let him watch telly because of his eyes, she had come in and read him stories every day, lovely stories, he still talked about them.

Mrs. Abdurrahman was said to visit Miss Gray fairly often, or send flowers and things; that big car blocked Mouse Lane. Ted Larkin had parked his bike across the front of it and hit the driver when he protested. The Abdus hadn't made a fuss, had been conciliatory. Mr. Abdu a very dignified man, local children afraid of him because he looked so fierce. Larkin too quick to hit out, he'd smashed Bert Farrell's car lights, had been in prison for fighting (GBH, and dates).

Mrs. Bates and Miss Pardoe, the vicar's sisters, had each separately heard Larkin having words with Miss Gray, once about speeding on his bike, the other time for an unknown reason. He had sworn most unpleasantly, had threatened Miss Gray "would be sorry" if she reported him. Miss Gray had wanted him warned for speeding, and Inspector Gurr had done so. Larkin's reaction: dumb insolence, then resentment at Miss Gray, for which the Inspector had further admonished him.

No one reported having seen Miss Gray after Monday evening. Bone wondered how the London police were getting on with Cryer's guest list. He had not much hope that any of the revellers would have seen Miss Gray plodding by.

7

AT the Bull and Oak, Bone would have liked something substantial for once, while all that was on offer were sandwiches, pre-packaged door-steps with a wisp of filling, or Ploughman's. He would have liked to have afforded another lunch at the Swan. He chose the Ploughman's. The labourer in question was acquainted with French bread. There was also a pottery bowl of butter, a sizeable chunk of very mature Cheddar, translucent white slices of onion, sepia pickle, and some rabbit-worthy lettuce. A tomato had been prettily quartered but, as always, had the fibrous core left in. Bone doubted whether the ploughman would have touched salad, or got butter with his meal.

They sat in a secluded corner that over-looked the pub garden, where tables had been tilted against a brick wall, and the flower beds sprouted dank chrysan-themums and distressed Michaelmas daisies under a valiant pink rose bush.

"So we'll see Mona, in case there's something in these imaginings. Carey Sidgwick says the house was locked against well-meaning intruders. And did she answer the phone."

"Otherwise it's a wrong number, with that outside chance that a child whose grandmother is dead would have answered it. Odd things do happen, though. Remember that Chief Constable a while back who picked up the phone and had a crossed line with two villains doing a transparent code talk on it?"

A couple had taken the next table, and the chat shifted to Locker's little son's football prowess. Bone from practice was able to talk about other men's sons smoothly, even about Locker's, much the age that the baby who died with Petra would now have been. Locker's early diffidence in mentioning his boy had gone. He had no idea it could still cost Bone anything to hear it.

Bone thought of Charlotte in her play on Friday. She wanted him to tell her aunt Alison not to come, and he had urged that Alison was interested. Cha, who already feared she had been given the part out of charity, quite violently said she wouldn't do it if Aunt Alison came. Bone, irritated, had accused her of being pettish.

He sighed, realised that Locker had stopped talking, and apologised. Steve said quickly, "Oh no. I could see you were thinking."

Bone looked at his watch. "Let's have another coffee and wait for Mrs. Staveley to be free at the Swan."

"If we have a coffee there, and we know it's good, we can be sure of catching her."

"Good thinking, that man."

They drove June Staveley back to Cross Lane. She was cheerful. The car filled with a dizzying aura of gin. Breathing it, Bone wondered if perhaps he shouldn't be driving.

Mona in the yard looked up through her hair. She was squatting before a construction of bricks, beer cans and large flints held together with mud. Her mother seized her, deplored her hands, the knees and seat of her jeans, all equally muddy and to the last of which she applied an instant remedy, promised her unspecified retribution, at which Mona smiled up confidently into her face, and threw the child before her into the kitchen. Mona fetched up against the table. Mrs. Staveley now discovered that the table was laid for tea and broke into praise of her daughter. She put the kettle on.

Bone intervened. "If we can talk to Mona for a moment, we'll be out of your way the sooner, Mrs. Staveley."

"You're not in my way, Mr. Bone. Time for a cup of tea, surely?"

Bone dredged up a winning smile. "We've come straight from lunch, Mrs. Staveley. You'll have to forgive . . ."

"June," she said expansively. "Call me June. Now, Mona, you answer properly and no stories."

Bone moved a pile of ironing from the sofa cushions to the sofa arm and sat down. Locker took a chair by the door, moving magazines. Bone tapped the cushion beside him. "Come on, Mona. Won't take a minute."

"You get a newspaper to sit on! If you put your muddy bottom on my settee I'll have the skin off you."

Mona obeyed, spread the newspaper and

sat crackling down, tucking her hands beneath her.

"How do you get into Nanny Gray's house when it's all shut up?"

June turned from the cooker, but Locker raised his hand. She stayed silent. Mona glanced at her, but Bone's note of admiration coaxed her. "I think you get in there. How on earth do you do it?"

Mona crackled dumbly.

"Oh go on, Mone. The policeman's not cross with you. Tell," June ordered. "Don't be a silly."

"By the cat door."

"Really? That little door? How do you manage it?"

"I scrunch through. It hurts."

"Where was Nanny Gray when you went in on Monday?"

"In bed."

"Which bed was that?"

"Her *own* bed. She never went upstairs. Just Mizidgwick went upstairs. She has a room upstairs but she lives at the Manor. Where Jem lives."

"I see. Why did you go to Nanny's house?"

"Dunno. For something to do. She

might give me a sugar sandwich like she did sometimes, or she might tell me stories. She knows all the stories there are. I asked her 'Do you know all the stories there are?' and she said if she didn't, nobody did. What happens to what's in people's heads when they die?"

"Mone, don't ask stupid questions."

"Nobody knows what happens. I personally think the ideas simply fly away. In Australia, the people who lived there long ago, before the white men went there, believed in a place called the Dreamtime, where thoughts came from. Perhaps the ideas go back there."

"I should think they do," Mona affirmed.

"When you got to Nanny's house, what did you do there?"

Mona paused. Bone saw he had asked too wide a question.

"Did you play with the cat?"

"No, I didn't. First I called and knocked. She was in, cos the shoes she walks in were in the box in the porch, and her garden shoes. I couldn't see in the bedroom windows because of the curtains.

147

I thought if she was asleep I could make a sugar sandwich."

Mona stopped as if gagged. The possible lawlessness of this had come to her. Her eyes slid at her mother and then at Bone, oblique and wary. June kept silent, either seeing no crime in the plan or doing her best to help the enquiry.

"I never had one of those." Bone's frank interest bypassed the guilt. "How do you make them?"

"Didn't you ever? They're nice. You get two *thin* pieces of bread," Mona's hands flew in freedom, she indicated the special thinness delicately. "Brown bread. Nanny cuts it herself, that's how it's thin, not like the shop cuts it. She has brown bread in whole lumps, not a loaf in wrappers, and you cut it and you put the butter on and you put dark brown sugar on." Her hands worked, the butter went on thinly, with care, the sugar thick, "And you put them together. Then you cut it in four for manners and *then* you eat it."

"I like the sound of that," said Bone. It sounded sickly to a degree, but Cha might like it. "So did you make it?"

"No."

"What did you find?"

Mona tucked her hands under her thighs and looked beyond him.

"The bedroom was all dark but the front room wasn't. There was Buffy on the floor and I talked to him and then I went into the bedroom and Nanny was laid on the bed, and I went to her and she was all still. So I went in the kitchen and I looked for the bread, only there wasn't none. And then in the front room the phone was off the thing, you know."

"The holder."

"Yeh the holder."

"Had Buffy knocked it off the holder?"

Mona, no fool, said scornfully, "It was on the top. The holder thing is on the table by the chair, and the receiver was on the desk; you can't knock a thing to be higher up. I sh'think Mizidgwick put it, not to disturb Nanny. So I put it on and I went and looked at Nanny. She was just laying there. And it was all quiet. I went and touched."

"How?"

Mona leant in a swift movement, picked up Bone's wrist from his knee and dropped it. Sitting on her hand again, she nodded.

"I see."

"Only it didn't move like your arm. It was all stiff like wood. It didn't lift up. Just the fingers was soft."

June, clasping a tea towel under her exuberant bosom, had come closer, but stood silent.

"What did you do then?"

"Oh the phone rang."

"Who was it?"

Mona swung her legs. The newspaper crackled. "Don't know."

"She doesn't like the telephone," June supplied.

"That's a pity," Bone said. "I should have hoped you'd answered it and then you could tell me who called."

"I did answer it." Mona was not proof against this method.

"Who was it?"

"Don't know."

"A man, or a woman?"

"Could of been a woman. Sort of a high man perhaps."

"Was the voice posh or ordinary?"

"Don't know."

"Mone! Don't be so thick. He means was it like him or like Ted."

Bone, not quite gratified to find his tone was posh, waited.

"Just a sort of high voice."

"What did they say?"

"Wanted Miss Gray."

Bone still waited, then gave a hint. "So you said?"

"Nothing."

"Nothing at all?"

"No. Nothing at all."

"What a pity. Then they didn't know who you were."

Mona shook her head. "M'm-m'm."

"You could have said what you liked."

Mona crackled uneasily. She said, "Then I looked for my glass flowers."

"Your glass flowers." Bone envisaged a Victorian posy. "Did you find them?"

"No. They been stolen."

"Stolen?"

"What glass flowers is that?" June asked.

"My glass flowers. What Nanny said I can have when she is dead. They was gone, and Nanny said I could have them."

"When she was dead!" June cried. "She

151

wasn't dead that day. You've no business going in and pretending things."

"What were your flowers like?"

"In a glass thing." Mona extracted her hands and made a rounding gesture. "Heavy. Hundreds and hundreds of little flowers made of glass, all different colours and like that, all little, with this see-through glass top. Nanny said I can have it when she's dead; and she's dead and someone's stole it."

"We'll look for it," Bone promised. He meant it. If they found a heavy glass paperweight, however, it would be likely to end as a police deodand. They very much wanted a heavy, rounded object to match to that dent in Phoebe Gray's cranium. "Where was it, usually?"

"On the desk. Sometimes Nanny would put it in the window but the sun isn't good for it, she mostly never moved it but to wash it and dust. She dusted a lot, even when you couldn't see no dust. I mustn't touch it without she's there, and I never, and now it's stolen."

Mona's affront was heightened by her sense of her own forbearance. She had done as she was told, and been betrayed.

"Don't you bother the police with your glass flowers, now. They have better things to do than look for them."

Bone thanked Mona for answering so clearly, and gave Locker one of their code signals as they stood up.

"If you're through, sir, can Mona show me what she was building in the yard? My little girl's a great builder too."

"That's right, Mona, show the policeman your play."

Mona raised cynical eyes to her mother, but went without demur. Bone said to Mrs. Staveley, "She'd done no harm at Miss Gray's, evidently. The cat door's bolted now."

"The little madam, getting in like that. And what a story, seeing Miss Gray dead."

"Children." Bone shook his head indulgently. "Mrs. Staveley, can you keep Mona at home for the rest of the day? There are people it might be as well she didn't talk to just now."

"Is she in danger?" June asked sharply.

"No, no." Bone was so hearty that, as he intended, she disbelieved him. "Of course not. We don't want her talking to people about getting into Miss Gray's house."

Mona had, it seemed, come blamelessly home after a brief search for her flowers. Bone and Locker went blamelessly off to the incident room for news. "A brief visit," Bone said. "We have to see that young woman at the Manor. I think I've got Mona prevented from going up there and tipping her off innocently."

"You reckon Mona's story is right?"

"Bar her not speaking on the phone. I think she did, and that it was Herne's call. She told Jem, and us, that she'd seen Nanny dead before. It's not a new story and I think it's the true one."

"And the rigor going off in the fingers."

They decanted themselves at the station doors. Bone's spirits sank as he entered. Even the collator was not Pat Fredricks with her pleasant horse face and calm, but a pretty blonde WPC whom he hardly knew and, as she was a pretty blonde, instinctively mistrusted. It was a facile opinion, he knew. Pretty women suffered from the cloud of approval in which they spent their lives. Some never learnt efficiency because they were perpetually forgiven their mistakes. Besides, he felt it was unlikely that a girl with such perfect hair and fingernails would be likely to have her mind on the job.

She stood smiling at him over the telephone she was answering. She reached for a package across the desk and Bone found himself noticing what this did to her skirt. She handed over a bulky transparent bag. Sealed, and labelled "Manor Woods" it seemed to be nothing but plastic. In fact, it contained plastic bags, transparent and smeared with lichen and less identifiable substances.

The girl rang off and said, "Pushed under a rhododendron and half buried in leaf mould, sir. It's marked on the map."

"It's a good find." Bone read the finder's name and gave the package back. "Let the team know that we're looking for a paperweight; multicoloured florets under a clear glass dome."

"Were you expecting this, sir?" She hefted the bag dispiritedly, and he gave a consoling half smile.

"We were beginning to."

A raised voice in Reception cut him off, a woman's voice, accustomed to servants. Berryman came in, thrown, to say in an apologetic mutter, "It's Mrs. Abdurrahman, sir. She insists, *she* says, I mean, that she insists, on seeing the person in charge about Miss Gray. She's making quite a scene, sir."

"Then it's lucky I'm here. Short of the Chief, I qualify as the person in charge about Miss Gray." He made a circular wheel-her-in motion with one hand. Relieved, Berryman backed out and presented Mrs. Abdurrahman.

An elegant woman, plumpness under control and rather suiting her, she was tall, in high heels too, wore twill trousers, a short very expensive sable coat thrown open, a wool tapestry shalwar, diamond ear studs, and chains on her neck and chest that would cover Bone's pension for a decade at least. The hand she offered carried a zonking emerald. Bone had never seen a stone anything like as large, and as his fingertips touched it he knew the unlikelihood of ever touching that amount of pure riches again.

Her eyes, deep brown and brilliant, were well made up but set in dark circles. Lines lightly bracketed her mouth, but it had nothing parenthetical in colour and opulence.

"Superintendent Bone?"

"Mrs. Abdurrahman. Will you sit down?"

She sank all her richness onto one of the tatty chairs, furling her coat close, and wasting no time. "I wish to enquire about Miss Gray's funeral. When will it be? You understand, I wish to order flowers in good time and also to be free to attend." Her fingers played with the edge of the coat, dived into the fur, smoothed it and let go. "She was a friend of the family, a greatest friend. We are all in her debt."

"The date depends on the investigation, and on the coroner."

"But in the case of accident surely? It will not be quite soon?"

Bone paused for a moment too long, and her sallow complexion paled as though a layer underneath had drained. She stared and then, in a curiously formal gesture, raised her hands to her face and stood up.

"Who could do this? Everyone loved Nanny so. To me she was a dear friend. To my daughters also. There could be no enemy of such a woman."

"You knew her well?"

"She was with me for Samira's and for Sayid's birth. Not as a midwife, you understand, but for myself and the child. She said indeed that she was not able, this last time, but I told her with no one else am I so content, so secure. I promised a nursemaid and all the help she can require. So she was such a kind woman she did not refuse. We were most happy. I am in her debt so much, I had wished to pay respect."

Male voices outside made her glance distractedly at the door. "It is my husband. I must go."

Bone opened the door. A dark hawk face turned towards him, a hawk beginning to go fleshy at the jaw and with a greying chin beard and moustache. The bleak gaze passed over Bone and looked at the WPC and at Mrs. Abdurrahman. Because a predator has eyes that in structure are quite like human eyes, one expects emotion in them, but they have none. In his own country, this man would expect police to act at his convenience and command.

Already at the door, with an anxious

smile, Mrs. Abdurrahman was speaking in Arabic, excusing and explaining. Her husband listened. The loom of his eyes swung to Bone.

"Murder?" he was dismissive. "What possible cause?" and having disposed of the matter he turned and left, his wife following. For all her furs, paint and jewellery she walked as if invisible in a chador.

The Manor's comfortable old-clothes beauty was a pleasure once more, with its appearance of having grown organically among its trees, putting out here a two-storeyed bay, here a porch with a small room above it, there a wing peering round the side. The outer door was open. An ecclesiastical damp stone smell met them in the porch. Uneven flags made footsteps echo. Locker rang.

From somewhere a response came, more a singing in the ears than a bell, but the inner door swung back almost at once and Mel Rees stood back to let them in.

Bone's foot caught on a flagstone's edge. He was fielded by an arm of pure muscle before he could fall.

"You're what's known as a useful man, Rees. Thank you."

"Lethal, these old floors. Miss Sidgwick's just coming. D'you wait in here?"

"Here," a smallish room, had a brick chimneypiece and hearth, matting on the wide boards and for furniture two superannuated sofas and a chaise longue, put out to grass here after a long life in busy rooms. There was also, by the wall, a metal clothes rack on casters, with wire and wooden hangers that shivered together at the door's closing. Locker took to the tattered leather sofa, Bone strolled to the window. Beyond his parked car, the drive swept away to the gates past the mown grass and cedar trees. It was well kept despite tyre tracks on the grass, and an unobtrusive panel radiator kept the room from being actually cold. Cryer had made the money, like the Hernes' distant ancestor, and to Bone's way of thinking had found a very good use for it.

The coat hangers made their tingling susurration and he turned. Carey's blue shirt, worn over her jeans, was crumpled at the waist as if she had been wearing a belt, or more likely an apron. Also in evidence was that air of social unease, like a schoolgirl among adults, sure of her own gaucherie.

"Mel should never have put you in here. What a fool he is. Won't you—"

"This will do very well, if you don't mind it."

"Me mind . . . Oh no. Of course."

She stood waiting, her feet together, her hands clasped before her. The face was open, enquiring, but the body contradicted it with defensive tension.

"Miss Sidgwick, we need to make quite certain, in the light of general information that has come to us, of some details, particularly about Miss Gray's injury."

She made no ado about going over it again. "Oh yes. Well, I was a bit hurried that day, with Ken's party, you know. I wish . . ."

"Can we go back a little further than that?"

"How far? When she first hurt herself, you mean? That was on Sunday night. She was sitting at the table when I came in, and she answered me rather vaguely. She said she'd had a fall, 'tumbled over,' she said. Of course I was worried, I asked about it and how she'd done it, but she wouldn't say a word except telling me not to fuss. 'Perfectly all right. Just shaken,' she said, but she did say I could help her to bed, so I did. She was quite glad to get to bed, I thought, but I'd no chance to look at her eyes or anything, she wouldn't have it. She said what she always said: 'I've been a nurse far longer than you, my dear, and I know what's what,' so I promised I'd look in again and she said I could come in next morning. She did seem better next morning. Oh, I forgot to say, I did go back that evening but she wouldn't let me in. Well, next morning she was watering the plants and feeding Buffy, she seemed better though she was slow. She said she would lie down or go back to bed, which worried me, but anyway I did her shopping for her. She hadn't finished her letters so I couldn't take them."

"She wrote those letters on Sundays?"

"She had this long correspondence with families she'd nannied donkey's years ago. It was an interest for her, I suppose. She used to get so involved. It was a bit pathetic, all these connections from ages

162

back that she clung to, but they wrote back, they didn't seem to mind."

When you're young, Bone thought, you don't need people.

"Then when I came in on Tuesday she did seem vaguer and I didn't want to leave her alone. She wouldn't let me stay, though. She said she'd take things quietly. She was impatient with me, and I couldn't make out that she'd had any breakfast. She got really cross with me. She said she was all right, and could look after herself, and I could go and make a nuisance of myself at the Manor. She could be unkind like that, but I knew it was just her age. She said Emily was coming later. I wish I hadn't believed her."

The brown gaze was fixed on the cedar, wistfully. "She'd posted her letters, so she must have gone out on Monday evening. Though perhaps she got someone to do it for her, Mona or one of the children, I thought. I hope she did. Only I'm not sure she knew what she was doing. I wish I'd been firmer."

Suddenly she plunked herself down on the chaise longue, pulled a tissue from her shirt pocket and blew her nose. "She wouldn't even let me make a flask of arrowroot." She blew again and then sat up with the tissue clenched in her hands between her knees. "Then next morning she'd gone. I tried to believe that she'd gone on one of her binges. But I must say Berryman wasn't helpful. He said it was early days to worry. It was Emily that got him going, she said that Aunty was in her seventies and had had a blow on the head. After that he did seem a bit more concerned. But they didn't really get any kind of search going until next day, and after all it was the children that found her."

"Quite. What food was there in the house?"

"What? What food?" She looked from him to Locker as if the question were so unlikely that she could hardly believe it had come from either of them. "What food? Well, I brought things in on Monday. Bread, and bacon, and kipper fillets that she was very fond of. And some tins I think. I was shopping for here as well, for the Manor, and collecting some things for the party. It's not easy to remember."

"What did she ask you to get?"

"I—she—" the eyes wandered. "I'm not sure. She was rather vague, and at one time she said she didn't want anything at all. I often did shop for her if she was gardening and didn't want to stop: then sometimes she would get so indignant if I offered."

"Did you check what she'd eaten, if she didn't seem to know? Look in the cupboards?"

Carey gave a short incredulous laugh. "Golly, no. It would have been more than my life was—" she clasped a hand over her mouth. "Oh dear. I wish I had. Only honestly I wouldn't have dared. It may seem ridiculous to you but you've no idea what she could be like."

"This happened earlier in the year, didn't it, Miss Sidgwick?"

She stared at him with her mouth open; stared at Locker; then glanced rapidly from one to the other. She had flushed. Then she took a gasping breath and said, "Oh yes. She'd done it before. It wasn't the same, you know." Then she broke into a short high laugh. "Oh dear! For a moment I thought you were saying it hadn't happened."

Bone stood up. "Thank you, Miss Sidgwick. You've been very helpful."

"Have I?" said Carey. "Oh good." She sounded startled.

Bone pulled off the road and stopped the car beside a field gate. Locker turned towards him, waiting, leaning back on the door with his arms spread. Bone, in unease he could not account for, said, "Substantially the same story. Right?"

"Substantially. I'll check it with my notes."

"Steve: where on a one-to-ten scale do you rate her credibility?"

Locker pursed his mouth and then shot out, "Six."

Bone had to pause as a farm truck thundered past, rocking the car and deafening them. Behind, its train of cars rumbled, then he could speak.

"Plausible rather than truthful. Now why?"

"Tone of voice? Or the eyes? No face-touching or any liars' signs of that sort."

Bone examined his memory of Carey

Sidgwick, standing, then clamped to the chaise longue. "Is she watchful? She's so fluent that she doesn't seem to be picking her words, but is she watching herself all the same?"

"I thought you might be coming out with the story of Miss Gray having been dead on Monday."

"If we had a more reliable witness than young Mona, and if the story wouldn't point to Mona, I might have done."

"There's Sir Valentine's phone call, if Mona would admit it."

"I could have pushed or manoeuvred Mona into admitting it, yes. I wish I could be sure that Mona couldn't be pushed or manoeuvred into saying nearly anything. Imagine Mona in the witness box?"

"Uh-uh. Sidgwick's story hangs together so."

"I'm going on the possibility that she's transposing Nanny Gray's fall earlier this year. She'd be convincing because she's sticking to the truth, and it'd be credible, six out of ten."

"You think she's the one, sir?"

"I think she could have done it. Opportunity, means, and probably motive if she's to come into her aunt's money; but that's weak unless we can find some reason for her wanting money at once and Miss Gray refusing an advance. We've got to go to court with more than Mona."

"Sir, would Sidgwick really not dare check on her aunt's injury, or whether she'd eaten anything? She's a trained nurse. Would she be that intimidated?"

"Perhaps it's family. Remember the doctor's family are the ones that always have colds."

"Policemen's kids get into trouble," Locker supplemented, and crossed his fingers.

Bone thought of Charlotte. Not in trouble, despite his long hours of absence, but lonely, stoically unhappy. Though she was solitary by nature, and her aunt lived down the road and her house was always open to Cha, yet she seldom went there: she was alone more than she ought to be. His job took most of his time and too much of his life. A few months ago she had said, with desperate and guilty honesty, "What's so awful is that I like having you to myself."

"Policemen's kids get neglected. As

to Sidgwick, Nanny was in the position of Matron. Her word went. Nursery autocrat."

"Evidently. So, the scenario?"

Bone sighed. "It's a ludicrous one."

"They often are."

"All right. Carey clubs her aunt, with presumably the glass paperweight, on the Sunday. Puts her to bed. Monday, does her shopping, keeps Emily out with word of illness needing sleep, knows Emily will be away on Tuesday. During the party on Tuesday she takes the body to the woods in plastic sacks, goes back to the party, and on Wednesday reports Nanny as missing. But why? Why delay? If she wanted to put her in the woods, and Heavens knows why, Monday would do. Sunday night would do."

"Hallowe'en, sir? Think there's a coven going?"

"I know damn all about witches, but that's a long way from home. Thanks for the idea. It's of a piece with the rest of it."

"Barmy. Did she think it'd be less noticeable on Tuesday, along of the party?

Cover-up, like? Nobody know she was up to something in all that to-and-fro?"

"With a mass of people milling around? I'm not so sure. Though it's likely the majority would not be in a noticing state."

"We've got her concealing a death, any way you look at it, no matter what the motive."

"Go over it with me: evidence she died on Sunday: abdominal contents consistent with Sunday breakfast at Mrs. Playfair's; haemostasis being previous to and inconsistent with the time of the animals' and insects' injuries. Evidence she was taken to the woods: plastic bags, not yet confirmed as having held the body. Evidence she was dead on Monday: Sidgwick did her shopping, kept Emily away, and may have impersonated her taking letters to the post after dark; also dubious evidence from Mona, possibly confirmed by Herne's phone call."

"I don't see but what that phone call has to be on."

"Suppose he got through to some Saxhurst child, and said 'Nanny?' and she said, 'Who?' and he said 'Let me speak to Nanny' and she said 'Nan's dead'. Far-fetched, you'd think."

Locker wagged his head. "Gets the slow handclap from me. Though I agree it's feasible. Mona showed a spot of confusion between 'Nanny' and 'My Nan'."

"I wish to Heaven," Bone said in a burst of irritation, "that grandmothers had never started this 'Nan' business."

Locker was diffident. "'Granny' sounds to me like a little old lady. My mother's earning her living, on her feet all day and she can run any of us ragged come the holidays, walking or sightseeing and that. I reckon 'Nan' sounds more active."

"I'm sure you're right," Bone agreed, annoyed with himself. After a faint embarrassed pause, Locker went on.

"Sidgwick might be trying to hide the cause of death, make out the blow was from a branch or a stone in the woods?"

"She must have more medical knowledge than that."

"She didn't have enough to prevent her from trying to hide the death, sir. She just seems to want to make out that it happened later than it did. There was that kipper fillets bit; if she knew her aunty had eaten kippers at Mrs. Playfair's, she needed to account for kippers in the intestine, so she said she'd bought some and that her aunt was keen on them."

"But there's more evidence than stomach contents about a dead body."

"She may not be up in pathology. What do nurses have to know?"

"People can pass exams in things and then forget them if they don't have to practise. Nanny was an SRN. Check Sidgwick's qualifications, and let's have a check on whether Sidgwick did buy kipper fillets on that Monday."

Locker wrote this down. "Though with self-service, the till girls don't remember the way someone might who's had to get it off the shelf themselves. They look at prices, not at goods and faces."

"Efficiency has made work a lot duller for a lot of people."

"I wouldn't be on a factory floor for the world," Locker said.

"I don't think the world's on offer this week," Bone said. "Now suppose Sidgwick knows medicine; does she know law? Would she suppose that if Miss Gray survived the blow and died later, she herself would be liable for a less serious charge? Manslaughter, as was?"

"Foster might come up with traces of her hair on Gray's clothes if she wore them on Monday, though there's less chance after all that time in the woods."

"Hairs. Strained seams? Sidgwick's a size larger as I judge it. Foster will have noticed. We'll have his full report tomorrow."

"She washed the bedding. That ought to eliminate traces of a dead body. There was a plastic undersheet on the bed anyway, so the mattress won't yield anything."

"We're still at the same point. Why this elaborate game? If she had put Nanny's body in the woods on Sunday night she'd still have appeared to have wandered there on her own, to have survived the blow."

Bone had the familiar feeling of his goal, of the reality, existing beyond a fog, of facts he could seize if he could only see them. He said, "We need facts. I want to talk to Foster," and he turned the ignition. "Why should Carey kill Nanny if she's due for the share of Gareth Herne's money anyway? She'd only to wait."

8

FIONA HERNE, the eye shield pushed up her forehead, turned the pendant in the clamp, held the arabesque of wire against it to be sure of its exact place, put the shield down, took the gas welder from its bracket and was about to apply the jet when Val, across the room, flung half *The Sunday Times* in a crackling cascade to the floor.

She swung the flame aside, said "Shit" and then "Why the hell can't you read that somewhere else? Isn't the house big enough?"

"Oh dear, oh dear. These creative spirits. What agony a work of art entails. Pity you can't make real money with these arty-crafts."

"I do."

"God, I mean real money, not a piddling thirty or fifty."

"Pity I haven't any real jewellery." She abandoned her work because it needed calm; crashed the welding gun on its bracket and lifted her goggles off her face and down round her neck. "All the family stuff Gareth didn't sell, you've hocked. Going by your mother's portrait I could have expected some very decent diamonds. They turn out to be thin-air-looms."

"How delightfully witty. But I didn't hock them, darling Gar performed that ritual to support his habit, and probably his crawling friends as well. He'd no sense of family."

"If he'd had a sense of family, my sweet, he'd have married again and begotten a quiverful of tots to put you out of the inheritance. That would enhance the position, wouldn't it?"

Val turned one of her metal figurines between his hands and put it down. He contrived to do it dismissively. Then he stared at her; his shoulders drooped and his eyes were tired. He sighed.

"We Hernes don't seem to excel at children. Gar and I only arrived after a string of miscarriages. Mamma had to immure herself in bed to make certain of a son and heir. And all for what?"

"Lucky for you she went through it

twice. You must at least thank her for that."

"Are you pretending, my barren darling, that existence is fun? There's a curse on this family and you know it."

"Not that again. Spare me the old, old story."

"Then *why* have you never had children?"

"If there's a curse on the family, far better surely that I haven't. And no more my fault than it is yours. In theory I'm fertile, and there's nothing wrong with your sperm count."

"As if that wasn't a humiliating enough business."

"Not a load of laughs for me either. I think this family is its own curse. Think of poor Gareth, adoring parents dead, Nanny left, shut up in the mouldering mansion with his disaffected little brother and a sister-in-law he couldn't stand. Not the luckiest life, and so no wonder he was always taking off. Which did him no good in the end."

"You were quite fond of Gar, weren't you, until you found you couldn't make him."

"That's the second old, old story. Trot them all out, pet, it may make you feel better. Let's have the one about everything in the nursery being always your fault, and Gar being sent to a good school and no money left for you. And what else? Well, you got your own back in the end."

"What d'you mean?" Valentine shot from his chair and strode up close.

Fiona began putting things away. Her concentration was gone. She yanked the drill's plug from its socket, spun the chuck ring and put the released bit into its slot in the case. Val's hand coming down suddenly halted her.

"What d'you mean, got my own back in the end?"

"Let go. You'll scorch your sleeve."

He let go. She turned the jet off. Looking Valentine in the eyes she said, "You were no good to him, were you? No help. As good as drove him to it."

She was aware of his tension. It would be safer to change the subject, to placate him. She reached down a box from the shelf.

"Look. I made this copy. Priscilla's

177

going to pay ninety-five for it. That's good luck, *non*?"

"One of these days you may get back the cost of all this expensive equipment."

"*Which* I paid for myself. Just remember that marrying me did your precious house at least some good."

"To have you mess up one of the handsomest rooms with your paraphernalia."

"Should I keep to arranging the flowers? I remind you that this is money and I'm good at it. People like what I make and what's more they buy it, and I can charge more all the time."

"They like to say to their friends that Lady Herne made it," he said contemptuously. "Without the name you'd be just another amateur dabbler with a bit of a gift."

Fiona held her tongue for a moment, then as he picked up her favourite pendant, an intricate cage of silver with a garnet caught in the mesh, she said, "So it's fine for you to spend days tinkering with old motors nobody wants to see, and dreaming up grandiose plans for showing a place nobody wants to visit. This is just one more hard-to-find little jewel of the eighteenth century, of a kind that England's littered with, no special charm and no special history, built by a competent nobody, the grounds never even sneered at by Capability Brown. I'm the one actually making money. That sunburst you thought so vulgar I sold last Tuesday at Ken's to Leo Tansley-Ferrars."

"Hope you see the money. He's quite the nastiest of Gareth's so-called friends. We're cutting off from that set."

"We are, are we? Where do I find such a good market?"

"Forget that piddling stuff. I need capital, a solid lump of capital to make a real showplace. You know that. You waste money on this—" he gestured, hit the clamp, and pushed it away furiously.

"Val, this is not Longleat. It is not even Polesden Lacey. It's lovely but it's not grand. It's not in terrific countryside. The house party scheme is fine, it's beginning to show we can do it, make a steady amount we can build on. The two goes we had show that. Well, I work my arse off over that while you swan around spreading the charm. I am not parting with capital for any Old Crocks museum. I've agreed to the bathrooms because those we've got to have. Americans in particular are not going to go on thinking it's quaint not to have enough of them. But no swimming pool and no fake water garden and no hard courts. We're not going to run a hotel. We couldn't maintain a pool and courts if we had them. That's off. That's final."

He was breathing hard, mouth tight and eyes wide and fixed. His hands jerked and he shoved them into his pockets. Finally he said, "Bitch." After a long staring minute, he wheeled and left.

She found herself making a gesture that was quite unaccustomed. She was hugging her arms to her chest.

The Manor kitchen was at first sight old-fashioned. Carey had become used by now to doors that latched. She took her apron from the back of the painted boards. Ken Cryer's predecessor in the house had had all the woodwork stripped, giving something of a Wild West look to the place. Sim had painted the kitchen woodwork white, and he had asked for, and been given, the modern stove and sink. He had hung dried herbs from the hooks on the beams. Ken suggested an actor he knew who would do for the ham to smoke in the chimney.

It was Sim's evening out. Carey extracted things from shelves, racks and cupboards; her hands moved automatically, her mouth was pursed in thought. Her inward eye beheld Bone's steadily attentive, inexpressive face. Why had he come to hear that story again? What was the "general information" that he had heard? What could possibly be in his mind that he seemed to question the truth of her story?

She organised the food into two parts, high tea for Jemmy and a late meal for Ken and two friends he was talking business with. She made celery sticks, the cheese dip, and was chopping cabbage, not with Pak Sim's terrifying knife. She rarely used his things though after all she had a right to them, they were Ken's really. She heard the children before they burst in, and they were quarrelling, which struck through her absorption. Mona's face was red. She leant on the table beside Carey.

Jem said, "You'll only get into trouble

if you tell the police stories. You're supposed to tell them the truth."

"Not stories."

"Monie, you know they are. You're not daft, stop pretending."

Mona's hand made a swift dart at the crudités. Carey as swiftly got in a sharp dab at her wrist with the wooden spoon. Mona tucked both hands into her armpits.

"And what stories is Mona telling the police?"

"I like Mr. Bone," Mona said. "He's sexy, isn't he? I think he's a dream. He looks like my favourite pop star."

"He's too old," Jem stated, "and your favourite pop star is my father and don't you forget it. There's dungeons in this house," Jem stamped on the bricks, "where I haf ways of makink you remember."

Mona ran at him. "You're stupid, stupid. Stupid bastard." They tussled. Jem held her off more than fought her, as she was uninhibited in combat.

"None of that. Stop it." Carey yanked them apart. If Jem's leg got kicked, Ken would be furious. She held each of them hard by an elbow, then thrust Jem away and steered Mona round the table. Mona had been telling stories to Bone, had she; and he had come asking questions again. Mona leant on the table and thrust out a quivering tongue at Jem, who used his hands to pull a horrific face. Carey to be casual went on slicing carrot sticks. Distantly the phone rang.

"Now, what were you telling Mr. Bone?"

"Su-per-in-ten-dent Bone. She told about Nanny being dead on Monday," Jem said.

Carrot pieces scattered. The children dived. "Bags!" Jem kicked away a piece Mona reached for. She kicked it back. Neither looked at Carey.

"Stop that. Both of you. Stop it."

Jem, the more amenable, glanced at her. He said, "Sorry, Carey. I keep forgetting it upsets you about Nanny."

Cryer's considerable voice at pitch called his son from somewhere in the house and Jem, still apologising, fled. Mona on her hunkers, chewing carrot sticks from the floor, raised her head. She saw Carey's face, and scrabbling up the carrot pieces she ran to the sink.

"I can wash it. I'll wash it all clean. I will. I didn't eat only one or two."

Carey came up to her at the sink, and Mona flung an arm to guard her head, and cowered. Carey took hold of her wrist and spoke to her. The water ran steadily and Mona did not take her eyes from Carey.

"Jemmy is right. He's quite right and you could get very badly into trouble if you tell stories to the police. If you tell any stories about Nanny to the police you will be taken away and put into a Home. I know all about the trouble you have been in for stealing. I know that you have stolen other things that people don't know about. If you tell stories about my aunt, about Nanny, I will tell the police and they will take you away and put you into a Home. They won't let you live with your mother any more."

The carrot dropped into the water and swirled to the drain. Mona continued to look at Carey, who said again, in the same tone, all that she had said. Mona was shivering. Carey as she talked rescued the carrot, put it on the side and turned off the water. Then she went back to the table.

"Run along. Remember. No stories, not even to Jemmy."

Mona belted for the door. The latch took three tries of her frantic hand. She got it open and was off, her footsteps diminishing along the flags.

Carey put small sprigs of watercress, delicately, among the celery.

Bone dropped Locker at the entrance to his block of flats, a nineteen-thirties building with windows round the corners, but with no other distinguishing marks. Locker's flat itself, seen by Bone only once, was jam-packed with furniture, with Joanna Locker and her mother Mrs. Pusey, two small Lockers below hip height, six budgerigars and two gerbils.

His own flat seemed roomy by contrast with his memory of Locker's. It was the top two floors of an old house, and as he came into the sitting room the setting sun, piercing the clouds for one of the few times that day, shone on the fitted carpet (inherited unwillingly from the last owner) and the battered brown sofa, the nest of tables, Charlotte's books on the floor, and an exhilarating bunch of chrysanthemums, red and gold, she must have come by during the day.

A sense of relaxation crept through him. It was Sunday. He was entitled to an evening at rest. He touched the cool edges of the flowers and bent to breathe in their autumnal smell.

The telephone shrilled. Not a duty call, he prayed as his hand picked up the receiver.

"Is Skelly in, please? It's Prue."

"I've just got in. I don't know, I'll call her. And listen, if you call this girl of mine Skelly, you can own up to *your* name."

"Fair enough, Mr. Bone. It's Grue calling."

"I'll tell her." He thought feet moved overhead. Out on the landing he gave their blackbird whistle and called, "Grue on the line."

"Co-ming."

He turned towards the kitchen, and as she came at a breakneck hirple downstairs, he said, "Nice flowers."

"Off a stall." She shut herself in with her gossip, while he put the kettle on and fossicked around, clearing the draining board, humming, eating a biscuit.

She came in as the kettle began to get excited, and pushed him away from it. "I make tea. Grue only wanted help, she is stuck in her homework."

"What a very utilitarian phone call. I expected the usual six months' duration."

He rejoiced that Charlotte was beginning to get over her dislike of telephone talking. She knew it exaggerated her thick consonants, her hesitations. Now at least she would talk freely with her own set. Taking messages for her father was another box of tricks, for she knew she must repeat the salient facts, the names, times, addresses, but to his admiration she turned off the answering machine when she was in. There was a courage in her battle with the enemy in her own mouth, the humiliating, disobedient tongue.

She snorted at his "six months" and put the teapot on its stand. He had found milk and some coconut buns. They sat in easy silence.

"Have you got s'evening?" she asked after a while.

"I hope so."

Hardly a minute after, the telephone irritably summoned.

"Mr. Bone, Fiona Herne. I'd like to talk to you. I think it's important but you could judge better than I can. I'm not at all easy about something."

"You'd like me to come over tomorrow."

"No, well . . . I'm not easy in my mind, do you understand?"

"You mean that it's urgent."

"I rather think it is. Yes."

And he heard that note in her voice. When you hear that note, you go.

"I'll be there at the inside of an hour, Lady Herne."

"Thank you. I'll be very glad to tell you . . . and will you come round to the terrace door? It's Palmerston's night off, and I can't hear the front door bell, and Palmerston can, and will answer, and I don't want him to have the trouble. I'll leave the terrace light. God, it's starting to sound like an assignation, but it's not."

"I understand. Yes." He hoped she was truthful. The last thing he wanted was an attempt on his virtue this evening.

"Thank you," she said. "Thank you very much."

He called the station, and he told

Charlotte, who shrugged and smiled, and waved from the window as he went out in the dusk to get his car again.

Dark had fallen thoroughly by the time he reached the Hall. His headlights touched the ghosts of trees, the grey grass and the strip of drive disappearing ahead. He pulled up in front of the house. A light on the side terrace silhouetted the gentle rustication of the corner stones, but he needed his torch for the steps, broken by frost and hazardous with the autumn remains of alyssum and rock rose.

The side door with its light had a rusty bell push. He heard the buzz of it, and Lady Herne opened the door almost at once. She was in corduroy dungarees of dark red over a purplish sweater, and a red paisley scarf tied at the nape over her hair.

"I can't shake hands, I'm filthy," she said. "I'm working. Come in."

9

LADY HERNE'S manner was reassuring, and she didn't appear to notice how very close to him she was in the tiny vestibule as she closed the door and switched off the outer light. She led the way. The dungarees had a layer of black on the right thigh at the back, in a shape that showed a hand was wiped there pretty often. Her fingers certainly were stained. Bone's wariness of an attempt to compromise him did not lessen, but he thought that at least she was not making an instant offer, an offer that in other circumstances he might have been pleased to get. It was her connection with the case that reduced her attraction to the level of professional risk.

"Hope you excuse my working, Superintendent." It was an assumption rather than a plea. "I've an order to fill, and these damn women won't realise these baubles aren't conjured from the air in the twinkling of an eye," the husky voice deplored.

Bone refrained from saying that the pretty objects lying on the table looked as if they had been so conjured. It was a personal and perhaps too gallant an observation. He rationalised it into "People who have never done a manual job can't appreciate the work it involves," and with this truism, leant on a chair back and looked around.

Half of a pretty sitting-room had been cleared for a bench. The room had a tinsel smell, the original metallic tinsel of his grandmother's Christmas ornaments, metal heated by the fairy lights of those long-gone trees.

She half-perched on a stool, bent to get closer to her work. She had her attention on something held in the padded jaws of a clamp, and at the moment worked with a magnifying stand, a big plastic lens on legs, like a crystal table. There was a small furnace at the end of the bench, and a tray of instruments at hand.

She said, "I should have made you a drink. Sorry. It's over there. And please sit down." She flashed a smile. "Find a chair, relax; take off your coat and your profession for the moment." She moved the object she was working on, donned an eye shield, and picked up the gas welder, whose minute blue flame played on the blackened metal. "It's pretty delicate. Not this, I mean, though God knows it is, but what I wanted to say. Basically, today it was borne in on me that I have money and that my husband wants it; and that my brother-in-law Gareth had money and my husband wanted it."

"Have you a reason to connect Sir Valentine's need with Sir Gareth's death?"

"I don't know if I have a reason or not, but I do have—what's it called?—grounds for suspicion. Hang on a bit. This is the awkward bit."

There was silence except for the gusting of the flame and her manipulation of wire. Then she began again, in the intermittent vague tones of one whose attention is occupied.

"In a while I'll make drinks, as you won't, and we can be civilised. She's calling for this in the morning on her way up to town . . . don't want to waste your Sunday evening, dragging you away from wife and family . . . Ken Cryer's party, the Hallowe'en do, he asked us I suppose because of Gareth, though I know some of that crowd fairly well . . . there's this snow queen, no names no pack drill, m'm? a thoroughly unappealing little shit even though he did buy a pricey bit of vulgar tat off me . . . not so much a black sheep, more a wolverine in black sheep's clothing, but good family, ha ha."

Bone thought: some Latin tag, about the worst of the worst being the best gone rotten.

"He cornered me. Came out with the Guinness record of the year for unlikely statements, that he admired Val . . . well, God! Val's in possession of a few nice ways, and most of our rows are over his loony obsession with this place, but admire? . . . This little creep was half-cut, or two-thirds, poor little sod. He said Val'd murder him if he knew he'd told. Poor little wreck was rather thrilled than otherwise at the thought."

She straightened up and put out the gas jet, raised the shield and parked it on her head, and wriggled her shoulders. The movement, slow and a little sinuous, was aimed at Bone. She smiled faintly, her eyes almost shut. Then she moved along the bench, once more at work although the smile stayed until she became absorbed once more.

"He said that Val had bought smack for Gareth. On the face of it, *the* world's least likely event."

Pulling her work across, she rearranged it. "Naturally, I gave him the raised eyebrows and the kind remark about in a pig's eye. After all, Gareth had money, however tough the trustees were with him. He always had enough for his amusements, and he could leave enough to Nanny Gray, God rest her; though I suppose it was out of the trustees' hands, when he died. Val said something about the damned trust being broken at last . . . But anyway, Val wasn't in any imaginable *way* likely to help him in his habit. I wish I'd a fiver for every tirade I've listened to on that more than dreary subject, and useless, I assure you, to explain to Val that saying all of it to me all over again was less use than a fart in a pig farm. But this man at the party said oh no, it was a fact . . . weird conversation, you know, with the party going on, and us shouting in each other's ears. He was white and sweaty and made-up and otherwise unappetising, but he had my arm in ye ancient mariner grip, and he smelt rather." Her face briefly contorted. "But he was earnest all right. He banged my arm on my knee and said 'Val bought Gareth uncut smack, cost a bomb and was about as bloody dangerous.'"

She picked up the little electric drill, loosened the chuck jaws and fitted a burnishing head. Her hands worked capably but she handled machinery with a certain violence, that was contained in concentration when she worked on the jewel. She put the visor down, reached out to the wall and switched on the drill.

She arched back and her breath whistled and shrieked in her throat. She stood jerking like a marionette with stuck controls. Bone hurtled round the bench, picked up the stool and used its wooden rim to thrust the wall switch upwards. She fell against the bench and dropped to the floor.

Bone pulled his sleeve down over his hand, grabbed the plug and yanked it clear of the socket, and as there was no room to manoeuvre between bench and wall, he dragged Lady Herne out onto the carpet. Her head was back and her mouth open. He pulled the tongue forward, found that her teeth were all fixtures, and started resuscitation. Her mouth had lipstick, which neither the doll nor the people he'd practised on had worn, but he pinched her nose and got his mouth over hers and breathed. Her open eyes made him feel she watched him in alarm as he worked; he swung from leaning on the breastbone to breathing, to leaning, to breathing; counting, checking, the drill he was thankful to have learnt, if only he could be sure he was doing it properly. Slow down, you're getting frantic. Better. Keep the rhythm. He looked for the room bell. All these big old houses had a bell in every room, surely? By the fireplace, it ought to be.

He had watched this done in earnest once, the young woman working on the old man on the common. A horrible old man, not clean. Lipstick was a minor trouble.

In case Palmerston would hear if he yelled, he used one of his deep breaths to roar "Help!" It wasn't a word that carried well. He breathed into Lady Herne's body, swung his weight onto her chest, breathed, shouted again. They didn't tell you that your back would start to ache.

Suddenly there was breath on his cheeks as he bent. The pulse stirred under his fingers. Her body woke to the pattern he was giving it, took on its routine. He sat back, a hand on her neck until he was sure breathing had established itself. He turned her on her side into recovery position, wishing the experts were here; you didn't know the questions to ask until you'd been through it. Her hair, tangled in red paisley, flowed over the carpet.

He saw no convenient coat or blanket to put over her. The only small rug was moored by a heavy chest and the end of the sofa. He put his mac and jacket over her and went in search of Palmerston, a telephone, or both.

He got them all but simultaneously. The telephone lay in the pretty room that opened onto the conservatory, and as he dialled Emergency, Palmerston in mufti of blue trousers and Aran sweater hesitantly appeared at the door.

"Ambulance." Waiting, he gave Palmerston an encouraging smile that probably more resembled a deathly grin. "Herne Hall. Yes, Herne . . . Hall. Electrocution. Detective-Superintendent Bone . . ."

Palmerston disappeared, and Bone hurried back to the workroom. She lay unconscious but steadily breathing, the pulse weak but unfaltering. Palmerston appeared with two car rugs.

"I have put the kettle on for a hot water bottle, Mr. Bone. I'm sorry not to have answered your first call, but I was not sure I had heard it."

"Can you help me move her to the sofa?"

Palmerston knew how to lift. They took hold of each other's wrists under her shoulders and her buttocks, and stood, and sidled to the sofa.

"It's a mercy you were here, Mr. Bone. I don't know when she would have been found. Sir Valentine isn't expected back tonight, and I would not have come in here this evening. It's my half day, you see. She might well have died, might she not?"

"It's possible," Bone said. It's certain, he thought.

"I will bring the hot water bottle."

"And Mr. Palmerston . . ."

"Sir?"

"Have you a fair-sized paper bag, or some wrapping paper?"

"Yes, sir." He marched briskly away. Though his face had betrayed momentary enquiry, his dignity of office kept him from questions. The hot water bottle, the brown paper bag, arrived in a few minutes.

"Would you stay with Lady Herne for a moment?"

"Certainly, sir."

Bone went back round the bench. He picked up the drill by putting the bag over it, coiling its cable in after it. He fastened the top with Sellotape from her bench and wrote on the bag.

"Was that the cause of the mischief, sir?"

"Yes. I'll get our electricians to look it over." He didn't say "laboratory". "I'll give you a receipt for it."

Lady Herne sighed and muttered. Bone moved the hot water bottle further from her feet. She was not yet of the company but her colour was no longer like dough.

"It's a real mercy, sir, you being here."

"Do you know how old this drill is, Mr. Palmerston?"

"No, sir. I never touch her ladyship's work things, and I have never really noticed them either. I do occasionally when supervising the girl who cleans in here, take a look at some of her ladyship's work. It's very delicate and clever."

"It's exquisite," Bone said. He put his fingers to her pulse, faint but steady.

"May I get you a cup of coffee, sir, or tea?"

"I don't think so . . . no, thank you. It's very thoughtful of you."

"Not at all, sir."

"Do you know who installed this apparatus for Lady Herne?"

"The Electricity Board put in the power point, sir. My book would show when, but it is several years ago. To my knowledge there has been no inspection since. Should I send for the Board's man to look at that point, sir?"

"It would be as well, and the young woman who cleans had better not use it until then. This may be the cause of the accident, though." Bone hefted the brown paper bag. "If it isn't, then the socket's dangerous. If there's a fuse to this part of the house, it would be a good idea to remove it until the check." He had no doubts at the moment, though Palmerston now said,

"The house needs rewiring, sir. That is one of the prob—the matters Sir Valentine is now considering. If you'll excuse me, sir, I think that's the ambulance. I have put on the front door light."

As he was waiting, Bone noticed the table round the end of the sofa: it held a tray with several bottles and a syphon, an ice flask, and pairs of glasses. He looked at Lady Herne. She had been business-like as she worked, but it was certain she intended to lead up to, or down to, something more sociable.

She lay with her mouth a little open, and her eyelids moved.

The ambulancemen brought in the stretcher. Bone identified himself and asked where she would be taken.

"Tunbridge Wells, sir. Won't be long."

It was not until he had watched the ambulance drive away and was about to follow that he remembered, and asked

Palmerston, "Where is Sir Valentine this evening?"

"I understood he was going to London, sir. Beyond telling me that he would not be back until tomorrow, he did not say. He probably told Lady Herne, sir."

He stood in the doorway, with the outside light on, until Bone had driven off.

Halfway across the park, Bone pulled up. He switched off lights and engine and sat there in the dark and the quiet, reeling down the window. He realised he had been breathing hard, and that his shoulders ached.

"You've had a shock," he said aloud, "Damn it, Robert, you've had a shock too." He relaxed, his jaw, neck, shoulders, back. He moved until he was sitting at ease. The air drifted cold on his face.

At last he drove on. He was haunted by the scene he had gone through: Lady Herne's rigid face, his labours. Her plan for the evening would hardly have included the kiss of life. Bone, not given to thinking women fancied him, knew when one did.

He tried to think, constructively, about what she had told him. Her husband, she said, was alleged to have bought heroin for his brother. Her source, not divulged, need not be reliable. He had intended to press her further to give a name, a person who could be questioned.

If Valentine Herne gave Gareth pure heroin, had he told him what it was? Would Gareth instantly inject it, would he recognise it as pure? Would he cut it to have more in the long run? What had the autopsy said? Bone hadn't looked closely enough. Was that the fatal overdose? If Valentine had provided that particular dose, he might have bought it as a sprat to catch a mackerel. Lady Herne thought so. It was a disgusting means to rid himself of a spendthrift incumbrance. He had apparently been so kind, in pandering to a habit he despised. Bone, used to human meanness, to the violent results of human egoism, hoped that this particular instance was not true. Lady Herne believed it was. She thought herself in danger, and immediately she had suffered a violent accident.

Look up the autopsy about the heroin. Talk to Narcotics.

Get the drill vetted by an electrician.

Suppose a man has killed to divert money to his obsessively loved house, and then finds that money is left to Phoebe Gray.

Motive, and method. Stop a bit. Would Nanny's death bring the money to Herne? Or would he believe that it might? Or had he been too enraged and vindictive to care?

Bone changed gear as he slowed for Saxhurst. The paper bag slid on the seat beside him. Suppose Val Herne had tampered with that drill. He must have heard from his wife that she meant to work this evening. He would have known that Palmerston was off duty and unlikely to come in.

Speculation, that Forensic could likely throw more light on; but if Val Herne could furbish old car engines or motor bikes, which must include the electrics, he might be capable of nobbling a small, battered electric drill.

This road into Saxhurst passed the side of Miss Gray's little house. A metallic glittering at the end of her garden made Bone stop, back up, and turn on his torch to see. Carey Sidgwick's Datsun was backed in on the hard stand at the garden's end.

She couldn't be in the house, which was sealed, so she must be visiting someone in the town.

The Staveleys' Cross Lane house was in darkness when he walked down to it. Then he made out a blue glow behind the curtains, and he knocked. After a moment, a window opened. "They're at the pub," Mona called. "Who is it?"

"Mr. Bone. The Police."

"Anyone could say that," responded Mona. "Can't let you in."

The window shut.

It was as well, of course, that Mona had been taught caution; but he hadn't missed the triumphant note, the glee at so legitimately defying the law.

At the incident room he delivered the drill, with instructions, "and I'm going to the hospital, then home. Any news?"

Berryman looked tired. "Nothing's come in, sir. The plastic bags have been collected, along with other stuff, mostly old rubbish from the look of it." He consulted a list: "Remains of pink chiffon scarf. Broken angle iron, rusty. Biro. Vacuum flask case, rusty, and broken inner glass. Metal spectacle case. None very near to the site of the body. And sir, the plastic bags, I saw some funny signs on them in some sort of blue marker, so I thought, well, I took a Polaroid of them, sir. Here."

Bone looked. Berryman had got a white background behind the transparent plastic, and the blue marker showed reasonably clearly despite the shine of the outer wrapper.

"That's Arabic," said Bone.

"I'm in for a bit of sarcasm, then. I sent a note with the bags asking if anyone could decipher the marks. They'll get very funny over me not knowing it was Arabic."

Bone rubbed his face. The Abdurrahmans did not fit seriously into any of his scenarios so far. "I didn't need Arabic," he said. Then, "That's very good, Berryman. Your own camera?"

"Yes, sir. I got my boy to bring it round."

"You did all right. Make a chit for the cost, and I'll sign it; they may allow it to you. That was good, Berryman. Alert."

Berryman looked remarkably less tired.

At the hospital he traced where they had

put Lady Herne. The ward sister was a small plump woman with irrepressibly merry eyes. Bone, who had been hospitalised for a few weeks after the car crash, heard from her with cynicism that Lady Herne was "comfortable". In the small side room she lay on her side peacefully enough.

"What had she been doing, Superintendent? Her hands were *filthy*!"

"Metalwork. She's a jeweller and sculptor." He turned from the door's glass panel and went on, "I'd like a confidential word, Sister—" he glanced at her badge —"Sister Faber."

"Come in here. I need details about her anyway."

Sister Faber was amenable to the request that Lady Herne should not be allowed visitors. "Though if you want complete security you'd better put one of your people here. We haven't the staff to keep people out if they mean to get in; we can just put off the casual visitor. Do you anticipate trouble? Or danger?"

"Her husband may make trouble when he's not allowed to see her. It would be inadvisable for *anyone* to see her, though."

"Don't worry, Mr. Bone. We don't want her upset either. Now, if you can help me with the paperwork about her?"

Bone complied. As he left, she was putting a "No Visitors" card on Lady Herne's door. He went home to do his own paperwork.

Sounds of Charlotte's present favourite record reached him as he climbed the stairs, and a rhythm of feet. This record was one of Bone's unsolved mysteries. A single, it had the same title both sides, but completely different music. At separate points on each side, the words were the same: he could identify *She turns me on, but I'm only dancing*. Admitting he knew nothing technical about music, Bone could still hear no similarity between the sides. Charlotte played either side impartially.

She and her friend Grue gyrated and wriggled to the more romantic of the two versions at present. They waved as he passed on his way to the kitchen, where he put on the kettle and began to write up his notes. As he looked at these notes it seemed to him, as now and then in his work it did, that the day had begun a very long time ago. "Lady Herne," he wrote.

The girls' voices combined in the lament: *She turns me on . . .* When the record ended he heard from the silence that the kettle's cut-off had taken it off the boil. He could not be bothered to see to it, and reached down a can of beer from the shelf instead.

He liked to hear Cha dancing. It was good for her coordination too. She hated both school PE and her therapy classes; the one was too public, exposing what she could not manage, the other too personal and often painful. He had urged her to speak to the PE teacher, but her acute self-consciousness hindered her. He saw she would have liked him to intervene.

It was one of the things on his mind.

Cha and Grue came seething in, crying "Supper" like gulls.

"The kettle's hot. Watch out."

"Were you having coffee?"

"Tea, I thought, but I didn't." He tapped the can. "This did as well if not better. I've these notes to get sorted."

"Daddy's Effing Reports," Cha told Grue. "Pay no attention."

Grue nodded her spiky head. "Carry on, Superintendent." She wore a crushed-velvet skirt, striped leggings, a striped football sweatshirt and several long necklaces.

Abstracting himself from their doings, as from the activities of the Station, Bone got on with his writing. He liked the noise they made. Grue, with her confident cockiness, gave the orders. Cha played insubordinate *sous-chef*. Presently there was a smell of toasting cheese.

A clatter announced that Cha had dropped the mustard tin. He glanced up, to see Grue restrain herself from diving to retrieve it. She let Cha do it, watching her awkwardness with an affectionate concern. He thought: children are often so mature.

Charlotte surfaced, and met his gaze. "Get on with your homework, papa. Even Grue's finished hers."

"You're joking." He bent to his task, and was deep in it when a mug of tea appeared beside him. He signalled thanks, took a grateful swig and went on writing. He had got through the worst of it by the time the welsh rabbit was nudged invitingly against his notebook.

10

KHALIFA had forced herself to be calm while she fed her son. There was nothing mystic about the effect a mother's milk had on a suckling child, when substances such as her adrenalin might permeate it. Certainly Sayid was fretful afterwards, so she sang to him, held him close. Nursing had in fact calmed her, and she drew in the delightful smell of him. He was her triumph, her vindication, and he was also, in himself, an adorable baby. She watched him settle into a doze, and his fingers made clutching movements on the skin of her breast. She admired the iridescent petals that were fingernails. At last, a son of her husband's blood.

It was absurd to dislike Hussein's visits to her husband. The cousins were similar in more than looks. Hussein had the same feral aspect, the same imperious temper. He was bound by the most sacred oaths to keep her secret, yet still she feared. She would always fear. A quarrel, say, and what might he not fling at Mahmud? Anger could override intentions.

Sighing, she wished Hussein would stay at home with his wives and sons. He might be in danger here if her other fear were true, and if he were in danger, then so would be her secret and herself.

She put Sayid in his crib, laid the quilt over him and left the nursery. The nurse-maid, waiting on the landing, stood up and slipped into the room behind her. A good woman, that, who knew no secrets.

Khalifa took her cashmere coat and strode out into the garden. She walked as if she could escape from an unquiet mind. Down the steps, between the rose bushes, through the yew hedge to the long walk where the dimness of cloudy moonlight let her see the stones before her feet. She paced there, one hand in her pocket and the other holding the fronts of her coat closed at the throat. If only she had been strong! If only she had needed no anaes-thetic when her children were born, if she did not babble so helplessly when she came round! At least she had found out that she babbled, in time.

After Samira's birth she had told Nanny

Gray of her despair: not that she remembered any of her random words, but only that she had held Nanny's hands and poured out words without ceasing, or so it seemed. It was her own unease that drove her to pester Nanny until, to calm her, Nanny had said that all she'd said in English had been her conviction that Mahmud would have daughters for ever. "You talked of chromosomes. Your studies have made you worry, Madam dear, but you can never be sure that a boy won't happen," and Nanny had with such kindness reassured her, told of families where a seventh or eighth child had been a boy; of husbands rejoicing in girls; of her own absolute discretion; and Nanny had repeated that most of her talk had been in Arabic, which she did not understand.

Back up the long walk Khalifa turned. She had ensured that only Nanny should be with her after Sayid's birth, because now she had something to hide. She had done what she must to ensure it would be a boy, and this time no one of her own faith or tongue should be present. Mahmud had indulged her, even to her surprise had gone out of his way to do so, telling Nanny that he would pay her double fees and, when she refused, that he would pay the fee to a charity of her choice if she would come. This Nanny could not resist, and when Khalifa thanked him he only said, "Women have fancies. You must be made easy at this time."

Had she spoken? Had she told Nanny Gray of Sayid's parentage? Afterwards, as last time, she had pestered Nanny to know.

"You spoke about the children and whether a boy would arrive. I told you often that it had been born, that he was a strong boy. But you know, Madam dear, people are quite incoherent when they're coming round, and if you had anything on your mind, be sure you didn't speak a word of it that I could understand. You spoke a great deal of nonsense, and most of the time you talked in Arabic."

Then it had all crumbled. She had heard Nanny tell one of the servants to go away in *Arabic*.

The words had dissolved her security, though Nanny again denied all knowledge of Arabic. She had not known the phrase was Arabic at all; she had "picked up" the phrase when nannying in Egypt, and used it automatically . . . but what else might she not have "picked up"?

Nanny, that good and kind woman, had brought her Bible and shown it to Khalifa. "This is our book, like your Koran. Now, you must stop worrying. I don't take oaths casually and I don't swear, but because you must stop worrying I'm going to take an oath."

The old hand with its knobbly fingers had been placed firmly on the black cover, over the cross in gold.

"I, Phoebe Janet Gray, swear before God that I do not know the secret concerning you, Mrs. Abdurrahman; that I shall never divulge that there is such a secret, and shall never in any way let it be known that I know such a secret exists."

She had picked up the book and kissed it, and patted Khalifa's hand. "There now, that makes you safe, so you must stop fretting, Madam, and think of the baby. This nonsense is not good for the baby. It will not do."

She had felt better from that moment. She had felt secure. Nothing, after that, could be too good for Miss Gray. She had so well understood—that strange, upright little woman.

The fault was her own, the blame her own. Why had she not been stronger? Weak, stupid, she had told Hussein that it was possible that Nanny knew.

Back down the long walk in the near dark she went, the stones hard under her soft shoes, the cold striking up. If only Hussein would go home, to those abundant sons, out of the way of that policeman's light, penetrating gaze. The shock had been dreadful. "An investigation . . ." what had he said? But they were investigating. It meant murder.

If only it had not been possible that Hussein had done it.

There was a brisk wind that Monday morning, carrying sunlit leaves across the road. Bone caught up with a horsebox on Goudhurst hill and had to crawl up in first, wishing he'd taken the other road. The horsebox, negotiating the turn at the church corner (one act in the continual miracle by which anything of any size got round that narrow angle) made him stop.

He looked up at the tower with its blue and gold clock face against the paler blue and the small cloud lonely as Wordsworth.

The horsebox turned off through a gateway not long afterwards, the dun rumps were trundled out of sight and Bone thankfully put his foot down. The car heater was on the blink again.

WPC Fredricks was in the incident room. Her smile didn't transform her plainness but cheered him immensely.

"Here's yesterday's house-to-house, sir: and Dr. Foster rang a moment ago." She put the typescript on his table as he peeled off his mac. "Would you like coffee, sir?"

"I've just had breakfast," he said, and then remembered that Fredricks could make coffee, and said, "I'd love some. Thanks." He fished out change and put money ready as he began on the typescript.

"Dr. Foster? Detective-Superintendent Bone." She handed him the phone, scooped up his coffee money and went to her corner where she had, as usual, built herself in with her bits and pieces.

Bone tried to follow the pathologist's detailed report, but it was conclusive. The probable time of death was up to a week before the time of discovery, certainly more than three days. The condition of the blood, of the stomach and organs, a whole list of things pointed to this. The depredations of the animals had taken place some time after death, not immediately. For some time after her death she had not been wearing shoes.

The plastic bags contained cloth dust and thread, some of it from the clothes she was wearing when found; hairs, faecal traces, lymph smears; on the outside, dried mud, and a trace of rosin, and Arabic letters equivalent to "Express delivery".

"My assistant, a very accomplished lassie from Iran," Foster said, "thinks they are likely a shop or cleaner's direction. The writing substance is more usually found in continental markers than in British pens. The bags can be got almost anywhere, they're for storage of full-length dresses or long coats. They look to have been used one inside the other, head-to-tail, and tied round with string at three places. I trust none of this supports your theories?"

"It marches with them nicely."

"Written copy on its way to you. And now you'll excuse me, I've more customers."

Locker, arriving heavy-eyed and late, found Bone staring at his notes. He apologised. His son had been sick most of the night.

"He and his mate next door found an unused pack of hamburgers in the pedal bin, and hotted them up on a bonfire or campfire they made. They'd been thrown out as past the sell-by date."

"Is he all right?"

"Sleeping like a baby. And I'd about dropped off again when Selina woke me going to the bathroom. *She* felt sick."

At this news of Mrs. Locker, Bone raised a friendly eyebrow.

"Yes, probably. She's wanted another. I don't know how we'll manage but she's so bloody optimistic. What's been going on, sir?—Thanks, Pat." He paid for the coffee Fredericks silently brought, and nursed the mug against his chest.

Bone, as lugubrious as he, genned him up, about the report from Foster first.

"So the bags were used as we thought? Sidgwick?"

"There is the Arab line, but so far no motive. A vague speculation of Mrs. Playfair's that Mrs. Adbad—Abdu—was placatory to Nanny. The bags could have come to the cottage on one of her presents. Pat, any more on that drill?"

"No, sir. I'll give them a nudge. No dabs on it but a woman's, or probably so, narrow and small, and very consistent, look to be all of the same hands."

"Drill?" Locker asked.

Bone was dialling Herne Hall. "God, yes. I had a lively evening. Here, read up on it." He gave Locker the notes, and rubbed his face with the receiver as he listened to the ringing tone.

"Herne Hall," Palmerston said. Bone identified himself and asked, "Is Sir Valentine in?"

"No, sir. He has not returned or telephoned. The hospital tells me that Lady Herne is comfortable and has been asking for one or two things, and I shall be taking them over there shortly, although I understand that I shall not be allowed to see her."

"That's right. Would you leave a message for Sir Valentine to telephone me when he returns?"

"I shall, sir, certainly. I have telephoned places where he might have been, sir, to inform him about Lady Herne; but he was not at any of the numbers, sir, though he had spoken to the husband of one of the people I reached, but she did not know what the call had concerned."

"Thank you, Mr. Palmerston."

"Thank *you*, sir."

"Could you give me that number?"

Palmerston gave it; and Bone, when he had rung off, handed the number to Pat Fredricks. "Ask them, in case Sir Valentine Herne should get in touch with them again, to ask him to ring Tunbridge Wells hospital where his wife is recovering from an accident. I don't know the number of the hospital."

"No problem, sir."

Bone finished his coffee while Locker read up the reports.

"So, we're off to see Miss Sidgwick, who has some explaining to do. This gives us more than Mona's iffy evidence. I don't place Mona among those who know what day of the month it is. I'll ring the Chief. And Pat, we'll need you along, please."

It was his intimation that he meant to make an arrest. He read through the house-to-house reports while Fredricks' relief was organised from the very short roster.

The bookshop proprietor: Miss Gray was noticeably less friendly after news about the inheritance from Sir Gareth got about. She had been very sharp about public talk over private matters. "The poor woman was persecuted, everyone asked her about it and reporters came. She bought more books. I think she felt she could be a little more free with money, though I don't suppose it would be in her hands yet."

Ron Barrett: Old Miss Gray thought herself a cut above people. Larkin had gone up to Mouse Cottage, shouted around the place and kicked the door when she wouldn't open up. He'd trampled the garden and finally relieved himself all over the front garden, "watered her geraniums". She told him she would call the police and he would be charged with committing a nuisance. Ted had cleared off, probably because he believed her and could not afford trouble. Ron Barrett had gone along for the show and thought it tame. Ted had threatened the old witch all the way home, nothing specific, just that no one was getting away with the way she treated Mona, and with hitting the kid, which was rich coming from Ted. No, Ted didn't abuse the child, just clipped her one if she got out of line.

Bone and Locker set off for the Manor. An Oriental voice answered the entry-phone, and the gate was opened, but an unknown bass heavyweight let them in; with a great deal of face surrounding his features, he had a neck as wide as his head. He thought Carey was out—"I only just got up. I'll go see—" and left them in the pleasant hallway. The carved chest had a vase with three chrysanthemums and two pine branches; their cool rich scent filled the place.

Cryer appeared, in very expensive, very old trousers and a Missoni sweater in moss green, indigo and ochre. He looked at Bone under the ruins of a very fashionable haircut and said, "You seem pretty hot for

Carey, Superintendent. Did she bop Nanny?"

"Is Miss Sidgwick not here?"

"What a po-faced profession you are in, to be sure. Sorry, Mr. Bone. Yours has to be a serious world. No, she's in London taking Jem to the dentist. Sloane Street. On to Peter Jones for an ice if he's able. They may stroll in the King's Road."

"There are one or two more things to consult her about."

"Helping you with your investigations?" The sardonic line appeared by the mouth. "Shouldn't think they'll be back before five and, come think of it, she may be later. She took her own car to Tee-Wells, and went on in mine because she planned to stop off there on the way back. Mel and Jem will be back sooner in any case, by lunch if Jem has anything nasty done." The eyes flinched. "But I don't expect it. Do I tell Carey to phone you?"

"That will be helpful," Bone said.

Cryer let them out, and ducked to peer at Fredricks in the back seat. "Carey'd make a pretty good policewoman," he said. "She doesn't seem to get involved with things and people. All this, for instance. Perhaps it's delayed shock and hasn't got to her yet but she gives me no impression of grief. A fraction fractious, but not what I'd call mourning."

"Nurses learn detachment," Bone suggested.

"She's not even in the same county. Nanny Gray was twice the woman. Jem is not letting on but he minds a lot."

"From what I've gathered, children would know where they were, with her. A woman of principle."

"Yes," said Cryer, turning his head to look Bone in the eyes. "Yes. Very much so. She told me where I stood, when I broke an appointment I'd made to see Jem in hospital. I've been bloody meticulous about such things ever since."

"I wish I'd known her," Bone said, and departed. He found Cryer a person who tempted him to converse in a human fashion. He would have liked to know him. The only thing they had in common, that he could see, was anxiety for a child not in health. Cryer might live unpretentiously but he was, after all, an international star.

"We'll drop you off, Pat, and see if Sir

Val has shown. I begin to feel that everyone I want to see is somewhere else."

"If you want to talk any more to Mona," Locker said as they passed Cross Lane, "she's there, larking about the alley."

"Not at school," Fredricks observed.

"Yes, pull up, Steve. If her mother's in, I'll talk to her."

"Want me, sir?" Fredricks asked.

"No, I think not. You both go back and I'll walk up there."

"I'll walk back," she offered promptly, getting out at the back as he set foot on the pavement. "I need some exercise."

"I'll park over the road and be with you," Locker said to Bone.

June Staveley at the washing machine said as soon as Bone appeared, "Our Mona's got an upset stomach, she couldn't go to school. I had to go out yesterday, but she promised she'd stay in like you said. She wasn't well when we got back yesterday evening."

Bone, thus placed as an Attendance Officer, said mildly, "Well, that's a pity, but it's convenient for me that she's at home. Is she well enough to talk to me?"

Mona had hared indoors as Bone descended the rubble of the lane. She was behind the armchair now.

"Come on out, Mone. Don't be a baby. The Inspector'll think you've done something wrong."

Thus demoted as well, Bone sat where June indicated, agreed that a cup of tea would be nice, and said, "How is the tummy now, Mona?"

"I've still got a pain," Mona stated defiantly, "and a headache." She brushed her brow with languid hand.

"Still, you were getting fresh air out there, which should do it good."

June lit a cigarette from her last one, and spooned tea into the pot.

"About the telephone call. You remember the telephone call when you were in Nanny Gray's house?"

"No." Mona sharply shook her head.

"You told us about it before. Someone telephoned."

Mona shook her head. "I made it up. I made it up."

"Mona!" June whirled and shot the word at her. "You know you're not to tell lies to the police."

Mona, wary, nodded over the chair back.

"Are you telling the truth this time?"

A vehement nod, the mouth tight.

"What about Nanny Gray, then?"

"I mixed her up with my Nan, like you said." She added fast "I made it all up."

"All of it? The sugar sandwich and the glass flowers? The lot?"

"Made it all up," Mona confirmed in a burst.

"You know what happens to girls that tell lies."

"I made it up, I made it up! It's not lies! I made it up." Her voice rose. "I never been there. I never seen her."

"It's all right, Mona," Bone said. June smothered the words she was starting, looking at him guardedly but tense. "You like making things up, do you? Stories about things? Stories you tell yourself? Perhaps you went in by the cat door another time?"

Mona eyed him. She gave a sidelong wriggle of indecision. "I might of."

"And Nanny promised you the glass flowers truly, or in a story?"

A definite sharp nod. "Truly."

"And they weren't there."

Mona drew breath. On the edge of Bone's trap, she teetered and backed off. "I never been there."

She was a good liar, sticking to the minimum, refusing temptation by compromise. Bone, an expert on lying, respected her steel. Why she had changed her story was another question.

"Mrs. Staveley, have you and Mona talked about this?"

"We've had a word or two about it. I mean, if she was promised something, glass flowers and that, she ought to have them, oughtn't she? I mean, she knows she had no business getting in by cat doors and the like, but she never did harm nor damage. She did take money once but she knows better now."

"You wouldn't get into any kind of trouble for going there," Bone said to Mona. "If you'd done any harm or damage, or if you took anything away, you might get a smack from your mother, I should think."

"She would," June agreed forcefully.

"Going in there doesn't matter. If you answer the telephone, it's all right. You

229

won't get into trouble about it. So will you tell me?"

"No!" Mona shot across the room and refuged behind her mother, seizing a handful of June's sweater either side and bursting into a series of frantic shouts. "No, no no no no no." The shouts took on a complacent fervour. *"No, no, no!"*

"Cut that out!" June tried to turn, to free herself, to get at her daughter. "You let go right this minute. Stop that. You let go or I'll give you such a dusting—"

The doorstep resounded to Locker's feet. At the same moment June managed to swing a clout onto Mona's ribs and then twitch herself free. "Ruined my top, you have. You look, all pulled out of shape. Clean on yesterday. Now, I don't want any more of your noise. Nobody hurt you. The policeman's told you you're not in trouble. I never saw you behave so stupid. Now, you be good and tell the truth."

In the middle of this scolding she shook the child, hugged her and put the hair back from her face lovingly. Mona raised to her a look of cloudy trust.

"Why don't you talk this over with your mother?" Bone suggested. "Have a word with your mother about what really happened."

June was listening attentively. She nodded. Bone stood up, feeling he had done the best he could for the present.

A clatter in the lane and a loud metallic noise preceded Ted Larkin. Locker side-stepped from the door barely in time as it opened wide; Bone made a forced *chassé* as Ted's helmet and gloves passed him on their way to the sofa. Ted had the makings of a black eye and was huge with rage. Taking in the presence of police, he at once set to, on full power.

"I'm laying a complaint. A formal bloody legal complaint against that poncing nancy and his bloody Roller and that frigging minder of this."

"What happened?" Bone asked temperately.

"Happened? What happened? I'll tell you what happened." Ted gestured, with a hand of the large economy size, first at Bone, then at the landscape in general. "I come up behind them on the Maidstone road and I passed them, and this lorry come round the corner so I had to tuck in a bit fast and that cun—"

"Mona!" June screeched. This invocation was addressed to Ted, who yelled, "All right! She's heard it from her mates at school. That bugger Jo Tench speeds up, dun he, and bam, I'm in the hedge. Then they come running back, 'You all right?' Oh, they don't want no charges, do they? They want to know I'm not injured. They don't want no bloody publicity and so I told them. Don't want your name in the papers for knocking a bloke off his bike, do you? And what do they make out but I cut in, and Tench even makes out he braked. Well, if he'd braked he wouldn't ever have touched me. Never. I'd the speed of him. He bloody speeded up. Had to or he'd never touched me. I'll get even with Cryer. Dancing about behind his minder. I got one in on Tench all right but he put me back in the bloody hedge because I got me heel on a tussock."

He was working his shoulder, then fingered his cheekbone with caution. Bone began to speak, but Larkin burst out, "It's easy enough, getting even with that lot. What about Lennon? And you seen 'Nashville'? All it wants is a gun at one of their concerts."

"No!" Mona yelped.

"Don't talk silly, Ted," June said. Bone decided that she was in the right; this threat could be taken as hot air; he noted it, and the nature that inspired it, but was practical.

"You could go up to the station and lodge a formal charge. What about the truck driver?"

"*What* about him?"

"As a witness."

"Are you bloody doubting my word?" Ted advanced on Bone and his right fist bunched. Locker pinioned him from behind but June seized an ashtray and flung it towards Larkin's head. Ash and stubs sprayed in a flying arc, the ashtray missed Ted by not more than a foot, hit the wall and thumped to the floor. Mona danced, her knuckles in her mouth. Bone, doused in ash and coughing, wiped his eyes, could not find his handkerchief, snorted and coughed again. June was exclaiming, Bone's eyes smarted and ran. He was aware of trampling feet across the room, and hoped that Locker had a good hold of Ted; he did not like the idea of being hit when he could not get his eyes open. He became aware that a damp cloth was being applied to his face, his hands prised away and the cool damp cotton put to his eyes.

"You let me do that," Locker said officiously. Bone, taking the cloth, got his eyes clear and saw Ted looking, regarding him with kindly joy and holding the end of the wet towel.

"I'm ever so sorry," June Staveley was repeating.

"It's all right."

"I never meant . . ."

"No harm done."

"Jesus, June, he can do you for assault."

"I only wanted to stop you—"

"Worked very well, too," Bone said. "An effective shot, all things considered."

"She stopped me all right," Ted said. He was simmering with the fun of what had happened to Bone. It had quite turned his temper. "You want to look in a mirror before you hit the street, Super," he said, and showed him the shaving glass by the window. Bone removed streaks of ash from his nose and chin.

"One day you'll regret that temper of yours, Ted," June scolded.

"I do now. I done things in my time I'm sorry for." He pulled from a pocket the size of a saddlebag a packet of Mars bars, twisted it open, tossed one to Mona and offered them round. When Bone declined, he pressed the pack at him. "C'mon. No hard feelings. If I'd hit you I'd be halfway to the nick be now."

"I dare say I'd be halfway to the hospital. Thank you; for my daughter."

He saw why there had to be a pack of the bars when one went to its doom in Ted's mouth. The family chewed companionably.

As he turned towards the door, Bone bent and retrieved the ashtray. As he did so, he saw a familiar blue scrawl on a plastic bag crammed with crumpled white cotton, in a corner by the wall.

"M'm. Where's this useful bag come from, Mrs. Staveley?"

"What? Oh that. That'll be off the coat I got at the summer fête, one of Mrs. Abdu's. She sends lots of things, really good too. The organisers get the best, of course, buy them before they get in the sale, but there's bargains. I got this lovely marocain coat in pink and black with a fur—"

"What's marocain when it's at home?" Ted demanded, obscured by toffee. "Sounds like anaesthetic."

"Marocain sniffing. It's the latest thing," said Bone. Ted's laugh echoed from the pan lids and the beams.

They got out into the lane, Locker helping Bone to shake off ash still. "Can't help being glad she threw it, sir. Larkin's a four-man job."

Bone wondered what that violent, good-natured man was capable of. He could have killed Nanny Gray in a spurt of temper; but packaged the body up and dumped it? Less likely. That could be still Carey's contribution.

If Ted hit her, Phoebe Gray would have dropped like an autumn leaf. His fist was his most likely weapon or, to a woman, the open hand; but you never knew. There was a masterless force there.

"One day that lad will be in real trouble," Locker said. He seemed often to have followed the same train of thought.

"We never got our cuppa," Bone said: but that was soon to be remedied.

In the Old Town Hall, organisers unpacked cartons, carriers and plastic bags (both black bin bags and the thick transparent Abdu variety) and were laying out trestles for the Jumble Sale.

"I suppose we should keep Miss Gray's system," said Mrs. Carren, a tinge of regret in her resonant voice. "It seems more respectful, this year."

"I should rather think *so*," Miss Pardoe replied. "In particular as there are some of her things here. I collected them on Sunday evening from her gate. I dare say she thought I had forgotten, as it was after dark."

"Do you think people will buy what belonged to her?"

"Why ever not? They bought old Mrs. Bellinger's things and some of them weren't nearly as nice as these. And we needn't *say*. It's all for a good cause, after all, and she put these things together herself, she meant the Sale to have them."

"Really we're just carrying out her wishes. Oh look, she's sent her pretty paperweight. Isn't that kind? One of her treasures, that was. Don't you remember, it sat in her window always?"

Miss Pardoe looked. "M'm-h'm. Not so very nice of her. There's a little nick in the top there. Cat knocked it down, I expect. She let Buffy climb on everything. It's smeary too."

"Throw me that duster, Cecy," and Mrs. Carren huh'd on the dome and polished it thoroughly.

11

"SUPERINTENDENT, Mrs. Playfair rang. She's got a Mrs. Wheatley there and thinks you'd like to hear what she says."

"Please call her, Pat, say I'm on my way. What about that electric drill?"

"Here, sir. Inconclusive, I'd say . . . Lady Herne's making progress. Sir Valentine rang Mr. Palmerston from London, and he's going direct to Tunbridge Wells to see Lady Herne, Mr. Palmerston says."

"Ah—"

"I checked with the hospital, sir, and she's definitely on the No Visitors list, still."

"Good." Bone read the report on the drill. Inconclusive was the word: the earth lead had come adrift; the live wire to the motor was frayed and touched the casing at its inlet; the grip insulation, a plastic layer, had been damaged and mended with plain adhesive tape, not the insulating kind. It was a thoroughly dangerous bit of machinery but there were no signs so far of deliberate tampering except that the screw heads showed they had recently been turned. All of it might be bad maintenance, but the frayed lead might show under microscopic examination whether it had been worn or cut.

"I'd like to see other tools in her workshop to find if they are in as bad a state or not. If they're not, this drill becomes more suspicious. If they are, Lady Herne had better be warned. Perhaps she had better be warned in any case."

"Think of that garage fire, sir."

"I'm thinking too of that electrocuted gardener at Saxden." He rubbed his chin with the edge of the electrician's report. "All right. I'll be at Mrs. Playfair's, Pat. Steve?"

"Do you suppose there's any of that cake?"

"Old Hollow Legs. We'll both be at Mrs. Playfair's."

He was putting on his raincoat when the phone rang again. Fredricks answered and said, "Mr. Bone, it's someone who thinks his car was borrowed from the Manor last Tuesday night."

"I'll take it." Bone said his name and heard a soft deep Scots voice.

"Simon Worth here, Ken Cryer's drummer. We've just been talking and he tells me that the old nurse lady may have been killed, poor body, on Tuesday night last."

"Was there something you noticed, Mr. Worth?"

"I think my car was borrowed. It may have been just a joy ride, mind, or someone that fancied a bit of rock and roll in the great cold outdoors, but when I went to load up in the morning, Wednesday last, there was a deal of mud on it. The wheels'd been through clay and there were thick splashes all along the sides. The mud flaps were fairly coated."

"Where was it parked that night?"

"In the manor stable yard first, then I moved it to the back drive. It's a big vehicle, you see, a Cherokee; there has to be room for a drum kit, and it was in the road of other visitors' cars. The back drive is a bit way from the main house but it's safe enough."

"And the keys? Had you them on you all night?"

"No. They were in the kitchen. I was in fancy dress and I'd no place for keys. Carey said they'd be safe in the kitchen, she or Sim would be there all the time."

"Thank you, Mr. Worth. It's kind of you to let us know. Where is the vehicle now?"

"It's here in Chelsea, and I've had it washed."

"Are you going to need it immediately?"

"I've a session tomorrow. I'll not need it till then."

Bone collected details of the whereabouts of the Cherokee and its keys, thanked Worth again and told him someone would be coming to examine the upholstery and floor; and saw Pat Fredricks writing down the details.

"Is it important, then?" Worth asked, interested.

"It helps to build up a picture of all that was going on."

"And there was I hoping you'd say, 'The final piece of the puzzle has fallen into place.' Ah well."

"A very interestingly shaped piece of the puzzle has just fallen into place," Bone conceded, smiling.

"That's grand, then. A man likes to be of use."

He rang off and so did Fredricks. She waved her notebook and said she would put in hand the collection of samples from Worth's car.

Going with Locker to his own car, Bone said, "So we have a large vehicle, big enough to hold a drum kit, that was parked out at the back of the Manor on Tuesday night with its keys in the kitchen."

"Still there's the matter of why the body was concealed so long."

"I think I've the key to that."

Locker's voice was constricted as he squeezed himself behind the wheel. "You have? What is it then?"

"I remember something Sam Pearsall said when I consulted him about Sir Gareth's will. Nanny got the money 'provided she shall survive me for thirty days.' Now if Carey expects Nanny Gray's money—get on with it, man; Mrs. Wheatley will have eaten all that cake—then Nanny must be alive for thirty days after Sir Gareth died. If Nanny doesn't inherit because she died too soon, Carey doesn't inherit either."

"Whew. Who does? Lost Dogs' Home?"

"The residuary legatee, perhaps. Sam Pearsall will know."

"It makes it unlikely Sidgwick killed her, doesn't it?"

"Less likely. The old lady could have got across her; given her too much good advice, say; threatened to cut her off; Carey loses her cool and bop!"

Fortunately Locker was also given to the camouflage of levity that Bone used. "Then she says to herself, 'Oops, a week too soon!'"

"And she starts the cover-up. Right. At the moment it's a question of, if she didn't, who did? Larkin? Or June Staveley, come to that, over Mona or even over Larkin's sins. I'm not keen on that candidate but she's not impossible. There's a long-odds horse: Mrs. Abdurrahman."

"Mare," Locker said, waiting for a truck to pull out from the garage on the High Street.

"Then Sir Val, livid at Nanny getting

244

his brother's cash." They walked up the road from where they could park, through the gate and up Mrs. Playfair's garden. Michaelmas daisies enjoyed a support system of planted twigs. Bone thought, "Petra would like—would have liked that." She hated plants tied to stakes. As usual now, his thoughts unobtrusively put her into the past tense after an initial moment of forgetting. The familiar small pang could, this time, be overriden by the necessity of responding blandly to Mrs. Playfair's greeting. As she opened the door, a cat, invisible until now, shot from the garden, jinked past the assembled ankles and raced upstairs.

Mrs. Playfair took them into her front room. Before the fire, her feet on the sheepskin rug and a cat on her knee, a very old woman smiled at them. She was a little wild-eyed, and her hair stood in vagrant white tufts, but she was neatly dressed in a russet wool frock and brown cardigan. Like many of her generation and of Charlotte's, she wore several items of incongruous jewellery, which she probably put on out of custom: small pendant earrings of actual diamond, a string of less genuine pearls, a marcasite flower-spray brooch on the cardigan and a diamanté poodle on the dress.

"There now!" Mrs. Playfair pushed a tea trolley into the centre of the group. "Time for elevenses if not past it. Sit there, Mr. Bone, won't you? Mr. Locker, the tub chair? Mrs. Wheatley will tell you right away what she told me."

She gave Bone tea without offering him sugar, and Locker with, showing an excellent memory. Her small bony hands moved deftly among the china.

"Mrs. Wheatley?"

"I told Emily all about this, you see, and she said I should tell you." Mrs. Wheatley was not to be accused of leaving out circumstance. "We were talking about poor dear Miss Gray, you see. A dreadful thing, her being done away with."

"Mrs. Wheatley lives at Mouse Lane Corner, Mr. Bone." Their hostess offered a good-sized plate of hot buttered scones.

"Not *on* the corner, but on the Sandhurst road, the one that goes on past the manor. It's not *on* the corner, it's more opposite Miss Gray's garden. Miss Gray would park her car at the end of her garden, because the road is level with her garden there but it dips at the corner. She did say, too, that it was not safe to drive out near to the corner. When she gave up driving, that niece of hers began to use the place for her car. Miss Gray stopped driving on account of her eyesight not being so good, and she said she was becoming slower. People said she drank, a wicked thing to say. She had an illness, and of course she didn't talk about it."

"Carey uses the car bay still," Mrs. Playfair nudged Mrs. Wheatley back to the subject.

"Other people do too. It annoyed Miss Gray so much! They seemed to think it was a vacant spot belonging to nobody. It *is* quite hard to park anywhere near the church, you know, because of the yellow lines, and people from the country house place—"

"Country House Hotel," Emily supplied in a mutter. "Mealden Park."

"—used it when they came to church, and the second time they did it, Miss Gray left a notice on their windscreen. I saw her do it. She was so cross! She pulled the windscreen wiper right away from the glass and then snapped it back on her note. I thought she had broken it. My son says, though, you can do that with a windscreen wiper. I shouldn't care to try. She had a car, though, before, so she would know you can do it."

"You saw her from your room," Emily prompted, heaving a cat's forepaws off the trolley and tapping its nose.

"Well, better from the passage than from my room, because of the lilac tree. You can't see across the road at all in summer, from my room, let alone across to that garden, and even in winter the branches are all in the way, but it's so pretty in spring with the flowers, it's a white one; and even in summer with the leaves, but last Tuesday I wasn't in my room at the time." Having unexpectedly arrived at the point, Mrs. Wheatley paused to take a slice of cake. "I shall spoil my lunch, but I don't care . . . I know the time of night it was, too, because I looked at my little clock because I could hear the noise from the Manor. Not the tunes, you know, but the drums. You can hear modern music a long way off, with the drums. It wasn't loud, but I could certainly hear it, so I looked at my little clock to see how late the party was going on, and it was past two o'clock. I wondered how the little boy could sleep, that lives at the Manor. Well then, I got up and went to the bathroom, which is what wakes me up at any time between half past one and three or so. I don't sleep the night through as I used to do, but I am thankful to say that I always wake up and always go along to the bathroom. My daughter-in-law wanted me to have a commode chair. She said my stick woke her up along the passage. Silly woman! Well, I paid for a good thick piece of Wilton, and my son laid it all down that passage. She can't complain now."

"And to do her justice, she doesn't. So you could hear the drum noise in the passage too, Marian."

"I dare say I *could* have done if I'd listened. I just went along to the bathroom. On the way back, though, I had a look out at the moonlight and there, right in Miss Gray's parking place, there was a great big thing like a van, with a bar across the front. I thought, she won't like that, won't Miss Gray; and I thought there was a light in her bedroom. It's downstairs and at the back now, because she couldn't manage those old-fashioned stairs. But I didn't see any more light, so I thought, Well! better if she doesn't know. And off I went back to my bed."

She reached her peroration with a rap of gnarled knuckles on her knee, and Bone said, "I'm extremely pleased you've told us that, Mrs. Wheatley. It's most helpful."

"Another hot scone, Mr. Bone," Emily said. Bone, aware from a pleasurable taste in his mouth that he must have eaten at least one, and with a vague sensation of having accepted more, looked at the depleted dish in embarrassment.

"Ought I? Haven't I had rather a lot— and without a word?"

Her eyes sparkled. "I was most flattered. I don't entertain handsome male visitors as much as I used to do, and you are picky about your food. Do you cook, Mr. Bone?"

"Yes. My daughter and I have found a common interest, and we experiment quite often."

She had beguiled him into a personal subject, and he turned back to Mrs.

Wheatley. "Did someone come to your house asking about anything you'd seen last week, or about Miss Gray and when you had last seen her?"

"My daughter-in-law said someone had been at the door asking questions."

Bone caught Locker's eye and resolved on a word to the house-to-house team. They, like the heralds with Cinderella's slipper, must not be put off until they had seen everyone in the house.

"Thank you again, Mrs. Wheatley; and Mrs. Playfair. We owe you both official and alimentary thanks."

She came with them to the door, picking up on the way a grey tabby kitten that was staggering amazedly down the hall.

"Daisy's child. I'm thinking of naming him 'Underfoot'."

"I'll get the car," Locker said, and set off down the path in the slight blowing drizzle that had started up. Bone turned to Emily Playfair, who changed the kitten to her left hand to offer her right.

"Mr. Bone, I hope we shan't say goodbye to you when this case is over. Does your daughter like cats?"

Bone's glance strayed to Underfoot, who

was sighting something in the garden. "We've been thinking of acquiring one, now that we have really settled in."

"Then you'll bring her to see me. That's good. *Au revoir*, Mr. Bone."

When he turned at the gate, she was waving the kitten's paw at him. Not everybody could have carried off so twee a gesture.

Pat Fredricks silently gave him a written telephone message as he came in. Locker put in the report on Mrs. Wheatley's news. Bone heard her saying, "Do you think it's all tied up now?" but he was reading his message and reaching for the phone. Then he had another thought and walked out across the parking lot to the station itself. The office was empty, and he shut himself in and dialled the number given: Charlotte's school. He was put through to the Headmaster.

"I'm sorry to call you, Superintendent, but we can't get in touch with Charlotte's aunt as we normally would during school hours."

"What's wrong?" Bone demanded.

"Oh, wrong—nothing is actually

wrong. There's been a set-to between Charlotte Bone and a member of the staff, I'm afraid." He sounded quite airy. "I'm sorry to say that Charlotte hit her, and isn't being very co-operative. It's not possible, I suppose, for you to come and talk the situation over with the staff concerned?"

"How is Charlotte not being co-operative?"

"She's refusing to talk."

"When can I see these people, this woman? Lunch hour?"

"I can ask them to be available then, yes. Strictly speaking . . ."

"Strictly speaking, I'm on duty, and in the middle of a case." Bone saw no reason to add that there were no further steps he could take in his case at the moment. On Charlotte's behalf he would seize any moral advantage he could muster. "Unless I ring again within the next ten minutes, I shall be at the school at one o'clock."

He rang off on the civil acknowledgements of this. The neutrality with which he had been working was blown. Cha wasn't talking. Didn't that hypereducated clod realise?

Striding back across the car park, he saw Locker at the window, and as Bone came in, Fredricks slid out and shut the door; evidently being tactful. Irritated, grateful, Bone turned to Locker. "Someone has stirred up Charlotte. I think I can leave things here for a couple of hours. Sidgwick's not expected until later this afternoon. If I say nothing's likely to happen, I enter the famous-last-words risk, but if it does, you can cover."

"Yes, of course."

"Don't cover up, though. If the Chief calls, tell him where I am. I'll get back as soon as I can."

Locker's demeanour was helpfully calm.

On the drive, Bone had to make himself slow down and cease apostrophising face-less schoolteachers. All the same he reached the school tense and seething. He was surprised at the normality of appearance of the man he briefly saw in reflection as he came up to the doors.

The headmaster was engaged, perhaps huffed at Bone's ringing off on him. The secretary showed Bone into an interview room which, except for wallpaper and a piece of carpet, he could have duplicated in any jail. Almost at once a short plump middle-aged woman arrived. Greying fair hair sagged round her face; trendy tinted glasses did nothing for her. She looked ill at ease and annoyed, not a charming combination.

"Mr. James will be here in a moment, Mr. Bone. We have an away match this afternoon, and he's having to ensure that all the team is together at lunch."

"Where's my daughter?"

"I've sent her to lunch." The woman dismissed the idea of having Charlotte present. "I don't want her here while we discuss her."

Bone drew breath and stopped. Reserve judgement, he told himself. The woman may be right. I doubt it.

"It's Miss Harkness, isn't it?"

"Charlotte's tutor. Yes. Please sit down, Mr. Bone."

"What happened?" He had no wish to sit down, but she did so.

"Mr. James will tell you what began it. I was not there at first."

A boy in shorts and T-shirt, who at second glance could be recognised as in his twenties, announced himself as Jim James and leant on the table with his hands in his pockets.

"Before you get out your truncheon, Mr. Bone, let me tell you I have not harassed Charlotte. I encourage her. I'm trying to get her to trust herself physically on the apparatus."

"Please give me the facts."

"Right, but I want to assure you there's no need to glower at me. I'm not unkind to her. I have not insisted on her trying what is beyond her at present."

"What happened? Please."

"It's a simple roll-over somersault. She starts well and then falls all over the place. I could see, as I watched, what was going wrong, so I had her repeat the exercise and I moved alongside and held her as she rolled, getting her to move the right way, and she reacted violently. She became quite hysterical, kicking and screaming. She couldn't tell me what was the matter. Prudence claimed that I hurt Charlotte, so I told her that I was sorry if I had but that she must calm down. She could only—well, I can't understand her speech easily, Mr. Bone, and she was more incoherent than ever, so I sent her to Miss Harkness."

"And I think that her behaviour over this incident is quite conclusive. I've said all along that she should be in a special school, one that caters for disabilities. We have no facilities here for the treatment she requires. We're not a psychiatric unit. If we try to treat her as an ordinary pupil, she shows that she cannot be so treated. She expects special treatment. Today's display was quite beyond what *we* can be expected to put up with. She kicked Mr. James and she hit me." Miss Harkness touched her upper arm tenderly.

"I'd like to see her now, please."

"She is at lunch."

"I'd like to see her, please. She won't be eating anything."

James looked at Miss Harkness, got himself off the table and went out, his plimsolls squeaking on the polish.

"The matter should really be discussed with the area authority's representative," said Miss Harkness.

Bone did not reply. He knew very well how to use a repressive silence and he did it now, on this obnoxious woman to whom Cha was merely an exigent nuisance. He regarded the table stonily.

"Charlotte could be catered for properly in a special school. She could have adequate speech training, for one thing."

He almost replied. He said, in his mind: my daughter can be goaded into incoherence by any unimaginative pompous fool. Children are vulnerable and, as a teacher, it's time you learnt that.

Charlotte came in. Her eyes were red, she had a wad of tissues in one hand. She crossed to Bone and stood close beside him, putting her forehead to his shoulder. He enclosed her with one arm. The PE teacher came after her and stood in the doorway.

"Do you want me any more? I've got an—"

"One moment, that's all. Cha, did Mr. James hurt you?"

She nodded. Her voice came obscurely. "Pulled leg. It won't go." She trembled, and Bone wanted to wreck the room.

"Mr. James, you've read the therapist's reports?"

"Certainly. Of course I have."

"I expect you forgot. I expect it's very hard for a healthy young man whose body will obey him, to keep in mind the limits that injury puts on a child."

"I had no idea it would hurt her."

"Yes. Charlotte knows that."

Charlotte nodded against his shoulder. Miss Harkness said, "Then there was no need for that outburst."

"She didn't know it at the time. Well, I think this has been blown up out of proportion. Charlotte will be able to apologise for hitting you, I expect, later, but I'm taking her home for the rest of the day. Have you got books and things to collect, Cha?" He heard the change of voice when he spoke to her. No doubt this Harkness woman would think him a doting idiot.

"M'm."

"You go and do that. I'll be here."

She touched his coat, and went to the door. On her way she stopped, and said with immense pains at clarity, "I am sorry, Miss Harkness." It came out with the hesitations and thick consonants, the blurring of a deaf person's voice. He had forgotten how badly she could speak. Miss Harkness made some ungracious acceptance, and

Cha went out. He said, "Don't let me keep you from your lunch, Miss Harkness."

"I don't take lunch. Do you think, Mr. Bone, that you could make an appointment with the Headmaster to discuss Charlotte's schooling?"

"Are you the tutor for the whole of the third year, Miss Harkness?"

"Yes. Doubtless you feel that she would be better off with someone else."

"Doubtless you feel the same. I want her difficulties understood rather than condemned. I shouldn't have been called in today. Someone should have been able to soothe Charlotte down. There must exist someone in this school who doesn't see her as a neurotic cripple."

Miss Harkness put up her head and was about to speak, but she changed her mind and walked out.

12

CAREY SIDGWICK had driven her own car to Tunbridge Wells and left it there in the car park, going on to London with Jem and his minder Mel Rees. She had made an appointment from which she could drive herself home, and for Mel it wasn't far out of his way. Jem still did not feel very well from the anaesthetic; his jaw was beginning to come back to sensation and he nursed it silently, lying in the back seat. He asked once, "Can't we go straight home?" but when Carey pointed out that she had to see Mr. Pearsall and besides, couldn't leave her car because she would be needing it, he subsided.

"It's not far, mate," Mel said. "We'll get you back quick." He glanced at Carey and added, "It's not far, Miss Sidgwick; we could go straight home and then I could run you back in time."

"That would take far too long. It's

almost on our way. Really, Mel, that's absurd."

"OK, Miss S. You're the boss."

So they had turned off the main road and bowled along under the great beeches, dropped Carey next to the town hall, and turned to go back.

She had time to spend. She had missed lunch because Jem wasn't up to it, but often she did not eat lunch. She walked down Mount Pleasant Street, pricing things and savouring what she was going to be able to afford.

Eventually it was time. She reached Mr. Pearsall's office exactly at the hour—and was kept waiting. The rattle of the girl's typewriter irritated her still more. The magazines were either about sailing or were cheap, women's rubbish. Carey put them back in their tatty heap and waited.

At last Mr. Pearsall showed out a pompous old man. They must have been talking social nonsenses from their tone. Carey got up at once and Mr. Pearsall stepped back, letting her in. After all that, he had to go out and talk to the typist.

Carey began as soon as he came back, seeing with satisfaction how his genial smile vanished when he saw she was not going to waste more time.

"About my aunt's Will, Mr. Pearsall. There's no point in talking round the subject, though I'm upset about her death and naturally miss her very much. I don't want to talk about that. I know my aunt left me a good deal of money and I've got a very good chance to invest some. A nursing home in Sussex is up for sale and it's exactly what I want to take on. How soon can I expect to be able to use my money?"

He had paused, and now he sat down. Fat was really very unpleasant—his chin spread over his collar and his waistcoat creased across his great stomach.

"Miss Gray's Will has to be proved first. We have to ascertain that it is her final testament, that she had her signature witnessed properly and that no other has been registered, you understand."

"You drew it up yourself, Mr. Pearsall."

"I drew up a will for Miss Gray, certainly. I sent it to her and she signed it and sent it back, and I sent her a photo-copy. But I have no knowledge that that is her final Will, or that she did not alter it or make additions or conditions. As soon as it is proved as her final Will, all monies left to you in it will be yours."

"What about an advance on it? I can now, surely, get a loan from the bank on my expectations."

He pursed his mouth.

"The same applies, Miss Sidgwick."

"But it's a certainty! Surely, Mr. Pearsall, it's only a legal quibble about some impossible possibility. My aunt didn't make any other will."

"I think you might have difficulty in raising a loan on expectations under an unproved will. Anyone who would lend money in such a case would be likely to impose very unwelcome interest rates to safeguard themselves, and you might find yourself in bad hands. Why don't you approach the sellers, Miss Sidgwick, and ask them how much of a hurry they're in?"

"They've had an offer. That's the whole point, Mr. Pearsall, they've had an offer, and I could beat it but they won't accept a promise. Would you at least be what they require: be my guarantor?"

"It's a thousand pities that this offer should arrive at this very juncture," he said. He had sat back in his pompous chair, as if withdrawing. "Your aunt would have lent you the money I dare say; and in a short time it should be in your hands, unless there is some hindrance. I don't say you can't approach the bank, but if it's the fairly substantial sum that seems likely, they may well give you this same answer."

"It's absolutely absurd!" Carey snatched her bag from the desk. "It's there, the money. My aunt survived Sir Gareth by a month, so it is certainly hers, and she left it to me and you know she did."

"I presume she did. I presume it, which is a very different thing. Miss Sidgwick, you're working for a well-to-do man. You might try for a private loan or advance."

"M'm." She seldom thought of Ken as being really rich, as he seldom spent much money. Indeed, the only big expenditure she could recall was the party, for which money had really flowed. The Manor was very comfortable, but not lavishly furnished; some of the rooms were even empty, and there were no thick carpets or luxurious things anywhere. It was surprising how nice the place looked, considering. "He might," she admitted. "I could try. This legal business still seems too cautious for words. I can't believe a bank wouldn't lend on such a certainty."

"Then you can try it. You've asked my advice."

I'll be paying for it too, Carey thought. "And you won't be my guarantor?"

"I'm not in a position to be, Miss Sidgwick, no."

"Oh, very well. Thank you, Mr. Pearsall."

As he rose, he smiled again. "If Mr. Cryer gave you a personal loan, he might not charge interest. Still, his lawyers might make difficulties too."

"Lawyers! Don't you think it's ridiculous to be so terribly cautious?"

"Wouldn't you want me to protect your interests by being 'terribly cautious'?" He opened the door. "I'll see if I can speed up the proof for you. That I *can* do."

Carey found that she had given him an automatic smile, which annoyed her as she had meant to show him how absurd she thought it all was. She passed the waiting clients without a glance, went down the stairs fast and pulled open the front door on Sir Valentine Herne who was raising his hand to the bell.

He was not as tall as she was and, let's face it, ever so slightly dapper, but he was good-looking, with thick fair hair and neat features.

"Hallo. Old Pearsall free, is he?"

"No. Someone was waiting. Two people."

"Damn. What were you seeing him about?"

What cheek! "Oh, I needed advice about Aunt Phoebe's money. Suddenly getting so much, I've got to be sure what to do with it."

He had been looking her over, but now his eyes became still. They were light blue eyes, quite large.

"So much, eh? That's nice. We can't talk here. Come and have a coffee. I've got time to spend, hanging about waiting to see my wife. She had a nastyish accident last night, got an electric shock from one of her crazy craft tools, and they're being tiresome about visitors at the hospital. It's all call-back-later." He was steering her down the street. "I was away in town, unfortunately. Trying to contact someone, a great waste of time as it happened. Rang up this morning and heard this news, quite a shock for me too. She's quite all right—" he hurriedly spoke as if she might think him unfeeling—"they're merely insisting on quiet."

Carey let herself be taken along. She too felt at a loose end, dissatisfied and annoyed.

"Might have a spot of lunch," he said.

"Not for me. Thanks."

The eyes swept over her again. "Ah, with your figure I don't suppose you do lunch. Women have amazing willpower. What about that place over there? Looks all right."

"Yes, they do quite nice coffee."

"A connoisseur of coffee as well."

The waitress, who generally installed Carey in a table at the wall by the coffee machine's roar and hiss, took them to a quieter table among the hanging plants in the relative calm at the back. Sir Valentine held Carey's chair before siiting down, and said to the waitress, "Two coffees."

"What else will you have, sir? We don't do just coffees in the lunch hour."

"Oh—coffee and cakes."

"Toasted teacake, sir?"

"Yes, yes."

"Black or white coffee?"

"Oh, black for me. Carey?"

"Black."

He chatted about the Hallowe'en party until the order arrived. He kept watching Carey rather than looking round the room. Two women at the next table dealt with chicken salad, and behind him a couple argued over which film at the Cannon they wanted to see. Coffee and teacake were put down and then he leant forward. He said pleasantly but in a tone she could hardly hear, "What makes you think Gareth's money is yours?"

She was astonished, and saw no reason to lower her voice as she replied. "Because she left it to me."

"She told me otherwise."

Carey drew breath. Did the fat old walrus Pearsall know that? Was that why he'd put her off? "*When* did she tell you?"

"Oh, when I telephoned her last Sunday."

"What did she tell you last Sunday?"

Still leaning towards her, he said the words in a low, very precise voice that almost seemed to echo Aunt Phoebe's tones. "She said that I would see that I had no cause to complain, as she was leaving her money where it would do most good. She thought that her Will was somewhat unjust, as the claims of family were not to be denied, and for that reason she intended to change matters, for justice's sake."

"For justice's sake?"

"An odd word, you think? She had a strong sense of justice, didn't you notice? She said that she had to consider you and your future. It was important as you were her only remaining family. So it was obvious that she intended to do more for you than she actually has done, but that she has left the bulk of it to Gareth's family. To me. Of course I'm sorry that she did not have time to make this alteration which would provide for you."

"Her Will did provide for me. I saw it."

Again he became still. "When?"

"After Sir Gareth left her his money,

she made her Will then. It's not three weeks ago."

"Then she changed it. She told me so on Sunday."

"She didn't change it."

The two women were glancing at them. Leaning towards each other and talking like this in low voices they must seem very odd. She was sure they must seem odd; she sat up, but when he spoke again he did not raise his voice and she had to lean over to hear him.

"Oh yes she did, my girl. Would she have said she thought she ought to provide for you if she'd already left you all of it? Oh dear no. It's a shame she didn't get around to that change she meant to make."

Stirred by this vicious little burst of spite, she pushed her plate out of the way and clasped her hands before her. He had made an enormous mistake and misunderstood Aunt Phoebe completely, and she was going to have fun telling him so. "She told *me* that you didn't deserve a penny of it. She said you were a cold-hearted, idle man. You'd been a mean and selfish boy, always whining for attention and always sorry for yourself, and you hadn't changed. And Gareth told her that he'd no intention of giving you anything and nor was she to." It was an effort to keep her voice down. She spat the words at him in almost a whisper. From the corner of her eye she saw the women's turned faces, their pretence at not attending to this smothered drama.

The waitress came by with a trayful of dishes. She put one down in front of the women, one between Carey and Sir Valentine: little cakes, in frilled papers.

He had been forced to halt as she came by, but now he lunged forward again so hard that the table shifted. His face was transformed, flushed and contorted. Her speech had struck home.

"She changed it. She told me so. She meant to allow for you, that's what she said. She meant to; but she didn't. So all your delays and hidings and pretending she was alive weren't much use, were they? All for nothing."

Even as he spoke he changed colour. She had never seen that happen so swiftly before.

"*Pretending she was alive?*"

He leant back, his eyes flickering. She remained leaning forward over her hands. If he knew Aunt Phoebe's death had been hidden, then he knew when it had happened. He'd been there on Sunday; and the only reason for leaving her for someone else to find, the only reason for not calling in help, not announcing her death, the only possible reason—

She began to speak fast, and so low that he had to come closer to hear her. It was worth telling him. She was delighted to tell him.

"She said to me on Friday. That Friday. That she had been feeling she'd been unjust. That was the word she used. She thought it was unjust to leave you nothing. She meant, she said, to provide for me very handsomely, but she thought that Sir Gareth's money, in spite of what he'd said to her, justly belonged to the estate. She meant to alter her Will partly in your favour. She was going to see Mr. Pearsall about it this next week. And I was perfectly prepared for that. It was her money and I had to put up with it. But when she told you 'the claims of family were not to be denied' you thought it was her family she was talking about, not Gareth's. You thought she was going to change her Will against you."

The table was juddering. She didn't know if his anger or hers shook it. A little cake in corset-pink icing slid against a shiny éclair and stuck to it.

"You thought I'd pretended and hidden her death for nothing. I did it so that she'd have survived your brother for thirty days and would inherit."

"But she didn't."

"Prove it," said Carey, and sat back. He was the only one who could pinpoint the time of Nanny's death, and he was the only one who couldn't afford to. Who better than the murderer to say when it happened? But his face did frighten her. After all, she was the only person who knew he was a murderer—a nasty sound, a word full of lurking and menace. Wasn't fixity of gaze the sign of a psychopath? She got up quickly and made her way out to the street. At that moment she half thought of going to Mr. Pearsall's, asking for paper and writing it all down, "to be opened in the event of my death" and telling Sir Valentine so. She glanced back and saw him finish paying and turn swiftly to the door.

She set off up the hill fast, turned at the bank, along towards the car park. She would get in her car and get home. If she told Ken that her life was in danger, he would see that one of the men went out with her. She ran up the slope of the road. As she crossed to the traffic island, she saw him coming after, nearer than she had feared. A group of people were walking round the foot of the car park towards the lifts and she went with them. The thought of running up the stairs of the nearest entrance, with him after her, was nightmare.

Round by the lifts there were plenty of people, both on the main stairs and in the foyer. She went up the stairs quickly. It could be difficult to get into the lifts when prams and a wheelchair were waiting. She climbed, with a shouting family, and came out on the second floor. It was unnervingly empty, but at least he wasn't there. She crossed the concrete, hearing car engines on the upward ramp along the centre aisle and round the far side. The lines of parked cars waited, and she stood back to let a car go by to the exit, then glanced to make sure no one was driving down the exit ramp before crossing the driveway towards her own little car. No one was on the ramp, but a car came round from the centre aisle. She was well into the middle of the driveway and supposed it would allow her time, at the low gear speed drivers used here, to let her cross. Instead it burst forward.

She stood for a second, then whirled and ran. She ran the way a car could not go, up the exit ramp towards the third floor, where cars only came down.

The car turned after her. He was mad. Obviously he was completely mad. She raced on. It was steep, but she was fit, and he seemed to have trouble at the corner and was held up. A good runner, she still did not believe she could reach the end of the long slope before he was on her. Incredibly his car was labouring, she heard the grind of gears, an engine's panting roar. He must be too mad to know what he was doing. Her pulse rasped in her throat and her legs hurt in every muscle. Round the corner she went and he was close now, but she flung herself over the raised kerb and fell on her knees by the wheel of a parked car.

His car came onto the level at sudden speed. To its left a big car was on the point of turning towards the ramp and he wrenched the wheel to the right. People shouted in fury and alarm. His car went headlong at the outer wall and hit it as its brakes screamed; but the rear of the car rose, showing its underside in one exhibitionist moment. The windscreen became a white fountain in the middle of which a dark shape flew out and upward, over the barrier, and disappeared in a long moment's silence before there were screams from below and an eruptive noise of breaking glass. The screams continued.

She got to her feet and, though her legs felt weak, she followed the people who were going to look over the wall. Down below were the bottle banks, which for some reason had not been emptied, and crates and rows of bottles were stacked along the pavement. Focus of hurrying people like an indrawing web, Sir Valentine lay on the shatter of glass.

Carey stayed there for some time. Then she walked down the stairs to the second floor and back to her car again, and sat there shuddering. She heard the sirens but did not move. After a long while she put the car into gear, and, still carefully because she was trembling, drove out along the concrete towards the exit.

13

THE phone was ringing as Bone brought Charlotte up the stairs. He had let her say nothing, only assuring her that he would sort things out a bit with the headmaster and that he thought Mr. James was all right really and would be more careful. "He doesn't strike me as a bad sort. I wondered if a woman PE teacher would have behaved like that and I dare say she would. When you're very healthy and fit, yourself, you can forget too easily."

"M'm."

"PE still scares you. I'll get a letter from the therapist and you can take it to Mr. James, and I'll get a word with him away from that concerned and caring Miss Harkness."

She said, "OK."

Now, as they heard the phone, she moved aside to let him go quickly up the stairs.

"Glad to catch you, Robert." The

Chiefs voice, apt to sound sarcastic even when he wasn't, grated in his ear. "Valentine Herne's in that case of yours, isn't he?"

"On the outskirts, sir, yes."

"Got involved in an accident in the multi-storey car park. Fatal, I'm afraid. Can you get there?"

"Is it immediate, sir?" He wished it was his old Chief, with whom he was on first name terms and who knew his situation. Charlotte made signals, and spelt "I OK" on her fingers.

"I dare say Sir Valentine will wait," said the Chief.

"I'm on my way, sir."

Charlotte picked up the raincoat he had cast aside on his way in, and held it for him. He rang off and went to her. "You rest, chick. I'll look in, or phone, before I leave for Saxhurst."

"Not worry. I do my word drill. Put my feet up."

She saw he was still worried, and she smoothed the frown lines on his brow. Tapping her chest with the other hand, she said, "Copper's daughter. No s-weat."

They hugged. As he was going downstairs she called, and he looked up at her leaning over.

"You were fine. At school."

He waved.

"Insane," the motorist said. "He came up the ramp—my God, you don't look for a car coming *up*. Fast, too. I slammed on the brakes, don't know how I missed him. I don't know how I braked in time. He slewed round and went full tilt for the wall. Never seen anything like it. Full tilt. I mean, lucky no one was walking. If there'd been cars parked there he'd have smashed the lot. What the hell could he have thought he was doing?"

Bone and the uniformed men, measuring the arc of the fall, wondered too. The screens and awning had hidden Valentine Herne's body but now the ambulance, backed into position, was ready to take him.

Bone had made the identification. One side of the face was almost untouched, but the rest was going to haunt him. What on earth had happened to produce this bizarre death? Had being turned away at the hospital made him fear that he was suspected of trying to kill his wife? Above rose the tiers of concrete, now lined with sightseers, particularly schoolboys out in their lunch hour, and crying and whooping like roosts of starlings. Bone's imagination hung that shape in its trajectory across the air. He hoped that the windscreen had knocked the man unconscious, dazed him at least so that he did not see, in that flying fall, what he was heading for.

They were having trouble getting to him through the glass; someone went to try for a broom at the back doors of shops. Someone swept with a cardboard divider from a carton.

The body, in the unreal light that came through the canvas, looked small, uncomfortable in its sprawl, and mutely patient. He might be his brother's murderer, his wife's if he could. He was, at this moment, a victim.

Bone was the senior there, but he had made it plain to the uniformed men that he was only an observer. Sergeant Easton's initial slight formality had given way, therefore, to good humour.

"No seat belt in use, Mr. Bone."

"Other witnesses around? Ones from up there?"

"The woman seems to have gone. Mr. Corrie . . ."

The motorist turned. "The woman, yes. She must have seen it. She was on her knees beside her car. She didn't have her hands up but I wondered if she was praying. You think odd things in moments like that. Just saw her in that moment. I suppose she'd dropped something and was picking it up. She came and looked over, just like I did, and she was very shocked. She didn't speak or hear me speak, and she went away after a minute."

"Can you describe her?"

"Can't say I can. Smallish, trousers and a light brown thing, short and padded, and she was very pale. I mean, one would be."

"I wonder if the checkout man noticed her," Bone said to Easton. "If she was very shaken, he might have done."

Easton sent a man round to the pay booth to enquire. To Bone he said, "Is there any reason that you know of why Sir Valentine might have a brainstorm?"

Bone pursed his lips and shook his head. "There are money troubles. He's got one of those big handsome old houses that cost thousands in upkeep. It doesn't make a likely reason for all this. I'd better get to the hospital to see Lady Herne."

Easton sent him a sharply sympathetic glance. They all had their share of breaking the worst news. "Hospital, Mr. Bone?"

"An accident last night. There's a distant possibility that foul play was involved, but I'm inclined to discount it on present evidence."

"Not a lucky family," Easton said.

Lady Herne had a dressing on her right hand, but she sat by the bed in her red cord dungarees. A jar of gladioli stood behind her head, giving an impression of brilliance and artificiality; the funeral wreath she had just missed getting? Gladioli always seemed to Bone like gardeners' flowers, unreal.

"Hallo, Mr. Bone. It's very civilised of you to call now, when I'm up, and not this morning. They told me you'd been, but I was *very* blurred and I'm glad you didn't come in." Her voice, husky and with that little note of mockery that makes a come-hither, was warm. "Perhaps you can tell me what did happen last night?"

She glanced at the sister who, when she heard why Bone had come, had accompanied him into the little room.

"I'm afraid," Bone said, "that I've bad news, Lady Herne."

"Oh dear, did Val—no, it's not a joking matter, is it? What's happened?"

"A serious accident at the car park."

"Serious . . . He's dead?"

"I'm sorry. Yes."

She looked at him, then through him. After a minute she said, "I suppose I'm sorry, too. I don't know yet. In the car park. God, he'd be furious. Always proud of his driving. I thought if he got killed it'd be on that foul little motorbike. He used to take it on the roads at night, you know. It wasn't licensed. But in a car park!"

She focused on Bone again. He said, "Would you like me to drive you home now?"

"Don't I have to identify him, or something? I'm sure on TV they always do." Before, he could answer she stood up. "I wanted to go home this morning, to ring Palmerston to fetch me. The sister let me know I'd better wait for you. Did he try to kill me, Mr. Bone?"

"The electric drill caused the accident."

"Oh. Very close to your chest. The drill was all right when I checked it after I dropped it. You saved my life, didn't you?"

"Very lucky I was there," said Bone, boot-faced, annoyingly embarrassed. "Is this your suitcase?"

"Always glad," the sister said, "when our guests walk out on us. Is there anything I can do, Lady Herne?"

"Poor Palmerston came all the way here with these things this morning and now I'm taking them back . . . It's normal not to feel anything, isn't it?"

"It's shock, Lady Herne. Shall I get your flowers wrapped?"

"No," Lady Herne said. "I'm not taking them. Is there someone who'd like them? I don't want them at all."

At first Lady Herne said nothing. She stared ahead, hands clasped on her thighs limply. As they were able to speed up after the log jam at Pembury, she said, "It was Gareth I fancied first."

Bone half-turned his face towards her receptively.

"Oh yes, Gareth was lovely—gorgeous to look at. Witty. He could light up a room when he came in. But he was hopeless when you got to know him. He couldn't be bothered with anything, even himself. He was useless about money; when his father was alive there'd always been all he wanted, then when his father died the trustees only allowed him peanuts and he scrounged on everyone. He didn't care. It was Val who had the go, the determination. That appealed to me. I found out a lot too late that Val's determination was strictly home-based. They were both like children. Gareth, though, Gareth wasn't mean. He'd stand you up and let you down, but he'd take trouble now and then for his friends. He went all round the county trying to find a house for Ken, and found him the Manor. He hated my marrying Val. Don't know why. He didn't want me himself."

There was silence for a while. Bone, not given to pretty compliments, felt one was called for, but she took up without rancour. "He was right, Val and I shouldn't have married. We were OK together a lot of the time but . . . you know, it's over. I can't get hold of that. It's actually over. Unbelievable. Last night, this morning even, I was his wife. Wonder what will become of the house? There aren't any heirs male, unless someone can dig up a forty-eighth cousin somewhere. Val made a hell of a song and dance about my being barren, but so far as all the damned tests show I wasn't and I'm not. And he was all right, no shortage. He said there was a curse on the family. Always annoyed me, his little dramas—but now look."

"Bad luck does seem to have arrived in big doses."

"Mr. Bone—hell, you must have a first name. Are you officially forbidden to tell anyone? I'm spilling my guts to you and you're called Mr. Bone."

"Robert." It was a forced concession. To state his own preference for formality on the case would be uncivil at this juncture.

"Robert. Thank you. Robert, what did actually happen? In the car park?"

"So far the reason for what happened

isn't clear, but Sir Valentine seems to have driven straight at one of the outer walls and to have gone through the windscreen. He had driven *up* the exit ramp. It was somewhat strange."

"Somewhat . . . ? He must have been in one of his rages. Oh shit. Poor little sod. I ought to be crying or something. Probably later, do you think?"

"It may be. Is there someone you can go to, or ask to come and stay with you? Your family?"

"Totally not my sort," she said. "Don't worry. Thanks for the thought. Palmerston and I will get by. We have a sort of understanding. On the basis, I think, of both of us trying to shore up the family in our fashions. He doesn't dislike me, which makes a change. Shit, listen to the self-pity. Well, why not? I can't be sorry for Val. He's out of it. Perhaps mourning is ritual self-pity time. Do you know, yesterday evening I meant to have a go at you? I really fancied you. It's gone sour now. Everything does."

She did not turn her head, but Bone's face clamped into its inexpressive mode. He withdrew from speculation on what he might have done. The strange deepfreeze his body had gone into at Petra's death might, or might not, have been overcome.

As the Hall appeared before them she sighed. "Wonder who it will belong to now. I never had the feeling of its being home. The dismal Carey gets all the cash there is. Robert: only one way to look at life—it's a joke, a bad one, but you can't offend God by not laughing, can you?"

Bone, beginning to notice that he'd had no lunch and that Emily Playfair's scones had happened some time ago, headed for Saxhurst and the incident room. He took the turning that led past the Manor, but the gate phone informed him in bass tones that Miss Sidgwick was not yet back. He drove on towards Saxhurst wondering more about a sandwich than his work.

At Mouse Corner, a car was in Nanny Gray's parking space. He stopped and backed up. Carey's, so she was back. Then he saw that she was sitting at the wheel. She had driven straight in, not backing as usual, and her head was down across the wheel, her fawn anorak bunched across her shoulders.

Bone manoeuvred his car into an inconvenient position across the entrance, as far off the road as he could get it. He climbed out, and edged along the passenger side of Carey's car. She had not moved; the door was locked, and he tapped on the window.

Her head came up, startled, the mouth ajar. Then she leant across and unlocked the door. He bent to look in.

"I've had such an awful shock," she said. "I don't think I'm quite myself because do you know what? When I was passing here I thought, 'Gracious, of course! I'll stop by and Auntie will look after me!' and I'd actually driven in and parked when I remembered. And I was quite, well, perhaps I mean overcome. Then I think I've been asleep, would you believe it?"

"It's quite usual in shock. You know that." Bone began to feel his métier was dealing with women in shock.

"Yes, yes. It hasn't happened to me before."

He refrained from telling her she'd had a lucky life if that was so. Bewildered, she seemed younger than she usually looked.

The dismal Carey? "Suppose you talk about it," he suggested.

"Yes. Please get in. I've got to talk to you."

"Let me drive you to the station. You can talk there."

"Are you arresting me? I do know it's a crime, but not a very bad one. Perhaps it's what they call a misdemeanour. I didn't kill her. Valentine Herne killed her. I only concealed her death."

"Carey Sidgwick, you are under arrest for the concealment of the death of Phoebe Janet Gray. I must warn you that—"

She covered her ears and said in a high voice, "Yes, yes, I know. I know anything I say can be used in a court of law. Just let me tell you. I'll say it all again afterwards and it can be taken down properly, but I've been so frightened. He was a dreadful, dreadful man. You can have no idea. He's dead. He couldn't be alive after going from so high into all that glass."

"You were there, then. Were you the woman on her knees?"

"Yes." She showed the scuffed and dirty knees of her trousers. "It hurts now. It didn't then."

"You had much better . . ."

"No. No no! I won't say *anything* if you don't let me talk to you now. I won't *ever* tell what happened."

It was a matter of personal judgement rather than sticking to the rules. He said, "I've a key to the house. Wouldn't you be more comfortable in there? You look cold."

"I'm freezing." She looked towards Mouse Cottage and began to clamber out. "Yes. We could put on a heater."

So they trod through the garden, which already with the energy of Nature showed a veil of weeds. He opened the door, turned on the electricity and, coming into the living room, found Carey pouring a fat finger of gin into a glass, then adding tonic. She screwed the caps on and put the bottles away. Bone reflected that a proper statement would have to be made later, but he did now manage to get in the formal caution before the drink could take effect. Carey waved a hand impatiently. She went to the electric fire and stood there, gazing at the Rayburn.

"Auntie was dead when I found her, with her head against the ashpan. I thought it was strange, because it was just like last spring when she fell over Buffy; but *then* she'd been wearing her hair tied up in a thick scarf because she'd been cleaning, and it cushioned her a bit. That time Gareth found her and called me from the Manor and we put her to bed. She was concussed, but she was all right and we were so relieved. But I think he told his brother what had happened. He must have done, because there she was last Monday, though I didn't know until today that Val had done it. I thought it was genuine, but he must have killed her and laid her there just like before. You see, he thought she was going to change her Will to leave him out of it, but she was going to change it to put him *in*. It's very odd that he ever thought she'd left the money to him in the first place, but it was probably something she said, because he got it all completely wrong. Wasn't it ironic? He was furious. I told him this morning. She was meaning to do exactly as he was asking, and leave something to him, but he killed her before she could. Half would have been mine, too, if she'd lived. He did us both out of it. It really came to me, when I was sitting there, what he'd done to us both. In two days more she would have inherited."

She turned to him, the brown eyes tragic. "Then I would have got it. How fussy d'you think they'd be? Don't you think they may not be fussy about just two days?"

Bone's immediate thought was of the Act preventing the miscreant from benefiting from the proceeds of a crime.

"Everything was much easier than I thought it would be," she went on, warming her hands alternately as she drank, "except for Mona, and how was I to imagine she could get in? I had to leave the cat flap as Buffy had to get in and out. I shut the bedroom door, of course, so he shouldn't get in there. You don't know what cats will do."

"Not the same as weasels and foxes?"

"What? Then on Tuesday it all went so easily. I'd meant to put on a mac over my fancy dress, but there was a pierrot suit drying on the radiator, so anyone who saw me wouldn't know me at all, with the mask, and it was so loose."

"And you used Simon Worth's jeep."

"Yes! You knew that?" She sounded

surprised, and paused a moment before plunging on. "Wasn't it easy? I brought it here, and carried her down the garden in the plastic bags. She was a bit heavier than you'd think, with her being so small. Then I drove back to the woods and found a place I'd seen before that I thought would be quite difficult to find, and I went back, and changed in the shed, and no one noticed I'd gone. How much of the money will capital gains tax take, do you know?"

"Did Sir Valentine say that he had killed Miss Gray?"

"He said she was dead on Sunday. And he tried to kill me. He drove his car at me up the ramp. Imagine! The wrong way up the ramp. I shouldn't have let him see that I knew."

She hesitated about where to put the glass, and finally put it down by the telephone.

"Didn't you," asked Bone, "feel any respect for Miss Gray's body?"

She stared at him. "Respect?" she said. "She was dead!"

14

"WOULD it be all right if I altered the name?" Charlotte sitting on the rug with a distraction of kittens held Underfoot against her chest and looked diffidently up.

"Oh, I would if I were you. It's only a milk name, you see. He's the one, is he?" Emily put out a finger and rubbed his domed head.

"It is not easy, but he is a one who likes me." Charlotte was at ease, as he had hoped; willing to speak, as she would not before strangers whom she felt to be critical.

Daisy came in, softly anxious, and when Charlotte surrendered Underfoot, she took him by the scruff and dragged him off. He was too heavy, but her hold made him bunch up his little body as she hauled him over the brick steps to the kitchen.

"Go and see where she's got them," Emily invited. Charlotte got to her feet and followed. Bone and Emily heard the squealing outcry, between protest and welcome, as Daisy and her burden fell among the other kittens in the bin. Charlotte too gave a small cry and stayed, watching.

"What happens about all the money?" Emily asked, fondling Mameluke whose light bulk stretched across her knees and the arm of her chair.

"I suppose the lawyers will argue that out. Carey doesn't get it. I'm not sure that, as Sir Valentine was Sir Gareth's residuary legatee, it won't go to Lady Herne."

"With the second set of death duties it will be a lot less than it sounded. I wonder if she'll sell that lovely house after all."

"There may be some distant male relative who will have to deal with that. Sir Valentine spoke of an entail."

"A ridiculous system," she said roundly. "If a woman can inherit the throne, then a woman should be able to inherit any lesser title and property."

"Did you know," said Bone, "that the Queen is a duke?"

"Splendid! Duke of what?"

"Normandy to start with; and Lancaster and York . . ."

"No," said Fiona Herne. "I have utterly no idea what will become of the noble seat. Sold off for debt, I imagine."

"And you, sweetie?"

"Well, I'll be sorry. It's a lovely place. Can't live there, though, even were it mine. Must find somewhere to set up my little workshop and carry on earning my bread."

"It's a funny thing," said Jay Tansley-Ferrars, "but Val was looking all over the place, the night before he died, for my little brother Leo. Where's your glass?"

"No more, darling. Yes, I know, but I'm ever so slightly off bottles, can't think why."

And she gave a neat, wry smile that set them laughing. She swirled the drink in her glass and thought: Val, you bastard, you could be very sweet. Not often, but you could.

"Did I tell you," she went on, "he perhaps tried to kill me?"

"No, my God, tell, tell." Camilla and Susan were enthralled. Jay went round pouring, and murmured his contribution of "Tell, tell."

"Well, I have this duckie little drill, like a dentist's . . ."

Khalifa watched Hussein's departure with relief. Their brief association a year or so ago had been as technical and cool as possible. He had offered no personal word at any time. She recalled his thoughtful imperious glance as he took in her oblique proposal, which she would have withdrawn, disowned, if he had looked at her body. "A duty to the family," he had agreed.

She turned back into the house, and climbed the fine sweep of the staircase, singing to herself. They are right to shut us up in the harem, she thought; we get into such wickedness. A duty to the family.

Ted Larkin gave a two-finger salute to the Cryer car as they met along the Ashford road. Mel Rees waved. Behind the visor, Ted's left eye sported a king-size mouse. He grimaced as he roared down the hill to Saxhurst.

"I got all your albums, Cryer," he said to himself. "In my dustbin."

He nearly took the feet off old Mrs. Wheatley at the corner.

Ken Cryer pushed open the oak door and whistled. An answer came from somewhere in the house. Satisfied, he looked in at the kitchen where Jo Tench sat with the newspaper, talking to the Javanese cook.

He picked up the letters from the hall chest. There were some for Carey, which he must forward to her friend's address, and one from her, which he opened at once in curiosity as he walked on into the terrace room. As he read, he paused, his mouth parted, and he began almost to smile. Then he grimaced.

Jem came in, butted his arm, got his head roughed about, and peered at the letter.

"Carey? What she say?"

"Embarrassing. She's saying here, Ta for putting up bail and that. So far OK. Then she's asking if I'll lend her quite a sum—see?"

"Coo."

"—to buy a nursing home."

Jem and his father looked at the writing, then at each other.

"It's bloody difficult to refuse nicely."

"Do you want to, then? Refuse?"

Cryer dropped into the sofa and put his feet up. "I do not, taking it all into account, think of Carey as quite the woman to run a nursing home."

"Don't worry," said Jem. "Shouldn't think they'd sell her one, would you? I mean there'd be a sort of feeling about who would she dump in the woods if it was to get her some money."

"I'd not have said that out loud myself but I did think it. No-o. My money is going to be inextricably tied up in next year's tour."

Jem sat on the sofa and wriggled until his feet too could reach the coffee table next to his father's elegant ankle-boots.

"I sort of liked her," he said. "It's not that. It's that I really did love Nanny Gray."

"What Sir Valentine evidently did," Bone explained to Emily, "was to come over here that Sunday night on a vintage motorbike he had, which was naughty in itself as it had no road licence. He tragically misunderstood her when she told of her intentions about the money . . . We've not so far found the weapon, and I suspect now that we never shall."

Charlotte negotiated the kitchen steps. She said, "Do you imagine 'Ziggy' is a good name for a kitten?"

In the church hall, Mona was pricing things with a professional air. She wormed her way into the front rank of buyers at this table and that. She passed the book stall without interest and reached a rather neglected table full of brass trivets, needlework bookmarks, wooden plaques with jokey poker work: Look busy, here comes the boss—together with pottery vases and souvenir mugs and spoons. Near the front by a shell-covered picture frame was a pretty millefiore paperweight with a minute chip at one side of the dome.

She leant far over the table and reached for some plastic fruit, turning it about. The stallkeeper glanced at the fruit and told her the price. "We haven't put the stickers on that yet, love. They're all the same money."

"Good, aren't they?" said Mona. "Really like." Under her open coat, her other hand closed on the millefiore paperweight with a slight chip on it, and when she stood up, the hand was in her coat pocket.

"I'll have an apple and an aubergine," she said. "My mum likes things like that."

THE END

GUIDE
TO THE COLOUR CODING
OF
ULVERSCROFT BOOKS

Many of our readers have written to us expressing their appreciation for the way in which our colour coding has assisted them in selecting the Ulverscroft books of their choice.

To remind everyone of our colour coding—this is as follows:

BLACK COVERS
Mysteries

★

BLUE COVERS
Romances

★

RED COVERS
Adventure Suspense and General Fiction

★

ORANGE COVERS
Westerns

★

GREEN COVERS
Non-Fiction

MYSTERY TITLES
in the
Ulverscroft Large Print Series

FICTION TITLES
in the
Ulverscroft Large Print Series

NON-FICTION TITLES
in the
Ulverscroft Large Print Series